THE VERDICT OF YOU ALL

BY HENRY WADE

Howard Coster.

THE AUTHOR

Henry Wade is the pseudonym of Major Sir
Henry Aubrey Fletcher, Bt., D.S.O., M.V.O.
He was educated at Eton and Oxford, served
as Captain, Major and Lieut.-Colonel with
The Grenadier Guards, 1914–1919. He was
High Sheriff of Buckinghamshire in 1925,
and has regularly played cricket for the
County of Buckinghamshire since the War.
Under his own name he published a full-
length *History of the Foot Guards*, and as
Henry Wade has written several detective
stories. His recreations are hunting, shoot-
ing and fishing.

PUBLISHER'S NOTE

If you are not already on our mailing list and would
like to know when new books are added, please
send in your name and address on a postcard.
Suggestions for new additions are welcomed.

THE VERDICT OF YOU ALL

BY
HENRY WADE

PENGUIN BOOKS LIMITED
HARMONDSWORTH MIDDLESEX ENGLAND
41 EAST 28TH STREET, NEW YORK, U.S.A.

First Published 1927
Published in Penguin Books JULY 1939
Reprinted DECEMBER 1939
Reprinted APRIL 1940

MADE AND PRINTED IN GREAT BRITAIN FOR PENGUIN BOOKS LTD., BY
WYMAN & SONS LIMITED, LONDON, READING AND FAKENHAM

CONTENTS

CONTENTS

CHAPTER I

"WHAT IS WRONG WITH SIR JOHN?"

" IF it's not taking a liberty, Mr. Jackson, I'd much like to know what you think is wrong with the master."

Mr. Jackson, thus directly challenged, drew slowly at his cigar and allowed a dignified but respectful frown to appear upon his fine brow. After a suitable pause, sufficient to suggest a reluctance to engage in gossip but not so long as to imply a snub to his attractive questioner, he replied, after the manner of lesser men, with another question.

" What, Mrs. Phillips, makes you think that there is anything wrong? "

The conversation was taking place in the cosy " Room " situated in the airy half-basement of St. Margaret's Lodge, a large house standing in its own grounds in that part of St. John's Wood which is so much more pleasant a place for wise—and wealthy—men to live in than is the noisy and overcrowded square mile comprised in the magic word Mayfair. Sir John Smethurst, whose wisdom and wealth were both beyond question to those who were aware of his prominence in the world vaguely but adequately spoken of as " finance," had yielded to his wife and been taken to live in Mayfair, but directly after her death, and ten years before this story opens, he had hastened to amend an error long since recognized and had moved northwards. He was now housed as comfortably as anyone can be in London, with a reasonable amount of air to breathe, quiet in which to think, and room in which to move.

The occupants of the Room were but two in number— Mr. Henry Jackson, the white-haired and venerable butler of tradition, and Mrs. (by courtesy) Phillips, thirty years younger than her companion, but, by virtue of her supremacy in her own domain, his equal in rank and privilege.

Mrs. Phillips blushed slightly at the austerity of the question with which her own had been met, but she stuck to her guns.

"Perhaps I shouldn't have mentioned it, but Miss Richards told me that Miss Emily was quite worried about Sir John, and she's not a girl that chatters, and so I thought there might be something serious."

"Miss Richards, of course, was quite right to speak to you, Mrs. Phillips, if she had to speak at all, and I know the subject will not pass into common talk. As it has come to our ears, I think, perhaps, I am justified in discussing the matter with you."

Having eased his conscience of any suspicion of gossip, Mr. Jackson prepared for a thorough and enjoyable indulgence therein. He settled himself more comfortably in his chair, and put his hand upon a neat decanter which stood on the table at his elbow.

"Another glass, Mrs. Phillips? A light and perfectly harmless wine, but of a rare bokay. I have no faith in a full-bodied vintage." (Jackson was quoting his master, but his companion was suitably impressed.) "You are right, Mrs. Phillips; there is, I fear, something unmistakably wrong, though I doubt if the fact has been discerned outside Sir John's immediate *décolletage*." (Jackson was fond of airing his French, though not always happy in his choice of words.) "I have observed it myself, and Mr. Hastings has spoken to me about it in confidence on more than one occasion."

"But what is it, Mr. Jackson? It can't be money, and at his age it can't hardly be . . . be . . ." Mrs. Phillips dropped her eyes becomingly, and the butler palpably ruffled his feathers at the challenge.

"If you mean love, Mrs. Phillips, age has nothing to do with it, and Sir John is, in any case, still a young man—younger, in fact, than myself." The butler was sixty-five, but he had a nice little sum laid aside in the bank, and both he and Mrs. Phillips were aware of the fact. "No, I don't think it's love, though. My opinion is that it

10

started about the time that South American gentleman, Mr. Fernandez, dined here about three months ago. You remember I told you he reminded me of that Valentino we saw at the pictures. He might have been a bit quiet before that—Sir John might, I mean—but that night, after Mr. Fernandez had gone, he seemed to me excited like, and since then he has been restless and jumpy. Not exactly frightened, but on edge—*excité*."

" What did Mr. Hastings say about it, Mr. Jackson ? "

" He didn't say much, Mrs. Phillips. Just asked me if I'd noticed anything. Said Miss Emily was worried about her father. Asked me not to speak of it to anyone—which, of course, I naturally should not do."

" It'll be a worry for Miss Emily, coming just now. And Mr. Hastings, too—a pleasant-spoken gentleman, I thought him. Miss Emily brought him down to see me soon after the engagement was announced."

" He's more than that, Mrs. Phillips. He's what they call a ' white man,' and I know Sir John thinks the world of him, trusts him like a son, more than——" He broke off as a bell trilled twice outside the door. " Ah, there's the study. That'll be him going." He glanced at the clock as he rose from his chair. " Eleven o'clock—earlier than usual. Ah, well, the earlier to bed for me. You'll be turning in too, I expect, Mrs. Phillips. *Couchez bien*."

Mrs. Phillips started.

" Good night, Mr. Jackson," she said.

As the butler emerged from the basement stairs into the roomy hall, the subject of his recent conversation was standing in the doorway of the study opposite, exchanging some last remarks with his employer inside the room.

Geoffrey Hastings was a tall, well-built man of some thirty-five years of age, with the greying hair and set mouth that came so prematurely to many young men who passed through the crucible of war, but the laughing, happy eyes of a boy. He was universally respected as a shrewd and capable man of business, but still more liked—it would

11

hardly be too much to say loved—both by women and men, for his capacity to get the full measure of happiness out of life and to see that others got it, too. It had, moreover, been revealed to him that even butlers and taxi-drivers had immortal souls, so that his popularity was not confined to people in his own walk of life.

He greeted Jackson, as the latter prepared to help him on with his coat, with a cheerful grin.

" That was a better bottle of port than I usually get here, Jackson," he said.

"Yes, Mr. Hastings," said the butler with a chuckle. " Sir John told me to get up a bottle of the '96 as he said he thought you might be going to bring him some news that you and he might want to celebrate. He said that last Monday, too, but if you'll remember, sir, you did not dine here, after all."

Geoffrey Hastings appeared somewhat surprised by this piece of information, but he made no comment upon it.

" Well, anyhow, Jackson," he said, " it did more credit to your cellar than some of the stuff you palm off on a poor secretary. Oh, by the way, Sir John told me to tell you that he was riding to-morrow ; he wants to be called at seven—a God-forsaken hour—and I suppose it means soon after six for you."

" No, sir ; Sir John won't let me get up early. James calls him. But I—I would willingly do that, and more than that, for Sir John, sir," said the butler quietly.

" I know you would, Jackson. How long have you been with him ? "

" Twenty-three years, sir. Ever since he started to be anything at all. He was a good friend to me, Mr. Hastings. I had been in trouble through a woman I was in love with giving me the chuck. He took me with a pretty rotten character—said we'd both got to make something like a fresh start and we might as well do it together."

Hastings laid his hand on the butler's arm as he stood in the open doorway.

" I know, Jackson," he said, " and you've only told me one side of the story. I've heard the other from Sir John. You've been a good friend, too. I only hope that I shall be as lucky when my time comes to start a household of my own. Anyway, early rising or not, it's time all hard-working men like you and me were in bed. It must be after eleven."

The butler looked at his watch.

" Five minutes past, exactly, sir."

" Well, good night and good luck to you, Jackson."

" Thank you, sir. Good night to you, sir."

The butler's eyes followed Geoffrey's figure, as it moved down the steps and along the winding drive, with a look of genuine affection.

" That's the right sort," he muttered to himself as he closed the door. " Pity there aren't a few more like him— there wouldn't be all this Bolshevism if there was."

And as Geoffrey Hastings disappeared through the drive gate into the street, a shadow gently detached itself from the bed of tall geraniums that bordered the drive and flitted into the blacker depths of the shrubs beyond.

CHAPTER II

P.C. RAFFLES ON THE SPOT

P.C. RAFFLES, of N. Division, was pacing in leisurely fashion down Regent Avenue, St. John's Wood, at about seven o'clock on the morning of October 28th, his mind pleasantly filled with thoughts of the hot breakfast and comfortable bed that awaited him as soon as his relief appeared, when he became conscious of the fact that his name was echoing down the silent street. Turning round, he saw a strange figure waddling down the road towards him, emitting at intervals between each panting breath the cries which had attracted his attention.

" Mr. Raffles !   Mr. Raffles ! "

On nearer approach the figure proved to be none other than the dignified butler of St. Margaret's Lodge, but in a condition hardly recognizable to his acquaintances. Mr. Jackson and Mr. Raffles had more than once shared a pint of port in the Room already referred to, Mr. Jackson being a diplomatist of the first water ;   but on those occasions the butler was clothed in the stately apparel of his office, to say nothing of the dignity thereof, his voice calm in the assurance of respectful audience, his face gently flushed by the generous wine. Now his appearance was very different. His face was white and haggard, with wild eyes seeming to start from his head on which the grey hair rose in a tumbled mass ; his body, shrunk to a mockery of the handsome figure which he was accustomed to present to the admiring world, was enveloped in a flowing Japanese silk kimono, evidently a present from his master, beneath which appeared pink pyjamas, one leg of which, hanging round his ankle, attempted vainly to perform the function of a missing slipper.

" Mr. Raffles . . . my master . . . Sir John . . . he's dead."

The butler leant against the neighbouring wall as he gasped out his message, but the stolid presence of the Law appeared to calm him, and he gradually recovered his breath and his equanimity.

" Dead, Mr. Jackson ? I'm sorry to hear that. Heart, is it ; or has he had a stroke ? "

" No, no. He's been killed—murdered ! "

The policeman at once began to take more than a polite interest in the butler's news.

" Good Lord ! Murdered ? Where ? In your house ? "

" Yes ;   in the study. Someone broke into the house last night. But won't you come and see ? "

" Of course I will, Mr. Jackson." The Law got slowly under way. " Are you sure he's dead ? "

" Oh, yes. No doubt of that. Dead hours, I should

14

think. But I told James to telephone to Dr. Bryant. I was that flustered I didn't like to speak on the 'phone myself. I saw you passing down the street from the study window, and I said to myself: ' This is a police matter. I'll get the police; James can get the doctor—he can't do any good, but he's got to be sent for.' "

" You did right, Mr. Jackson. Is that chap going in at your gate ? "

" Ah, that is Dr. Bryant."

The police constable at once broke into a run.

" He mustn't touch that body without me present," he jerked out.

His fear was groundless, as the doctor was only just being admitted to the house by the footman as he came panting up to the steps.

" Good morning, officer," said Dr. Bryant. " Are we the first on the scene ? "

" Yes, sir, as far as I know. The butler was just fetching me when I saw you arrive. It was my duty to see that the body wasn't moved, sir, so I put on a bit of extra speed."

" That's all right, officer; I know the routine in these cases. Now then, where's the body ? "

They turned to the butler, who was just entering the house. He led them to the door of the study on the right-hand side of the entrance hall, and turned the key.

" Hullo, door locked ? " said the constable.

" Yes, sir; I locked it," replied the butler, " to make sure no one came into the room while I was out fetching you. I didn't touch the window or let anyone stand outside it—I thought it might upset possible clues."

" Right again, Mr. Jackson. Pity there aren't more like you. But was the door locked when the body was found ? "

" I think not, sir. But Alice, the head-housemaid, will tell you about that; she found the body."

" Right; then we'll go in."

15

The three men entered the room, in which the electric
light was still burning, the butler closing the door after
them and remaining by it. The other two at once walked
across to the body, which was lying face downwards between
the writing-table and one of the French windows. The
doctor knelt down beside it, whilst the policeman established himself in a commanding position at its feet, from
which he could see that mere Medicine should in no way
interfere with the ordered course of the Law. But Dr.
Bryant, as he had said, knew the routine in these cases.
A glance at the skin had been enough to confirm the fact
of death, but as a matter of routine he touched the wrist
and held a watch-glass to the small amount of mouth and
nostril which was visible. After closely scrutinizing the
back of the dead man's head and gently feeling it with his
sensitive fingers, the doctor rose to his feet and turned to
the constable.

"Yes, dead several hours. Fractured base of skull, I
should think. Of course, a proper examination must be
made, but no doubt your divisional surgeon will wish to
do that. Oh, by the way, Jackson, what about Miss
Smethurst? Is she away?"

"No, sir. I have not yet informed Miss Emily of the
contretemps. As there was no doubt as to Sir John being
dead, I thought it best not to bring her upon the scene
until the police were in charge. ("Ain't he a bloody little
pearl?" P.C. Raffles murmured into his moustache.) I
propose with your permission to ring up Mr. Hastings,
her fiance and Sir John's secretary, and ask him to break
the sad news to her."

The doctor, inwardly calling the butler a cold-blooded
old fish, shrugged his shoulders.

"Very well, Jackson," he said. "I dare say you're
right. Well, I must be off. Shall be at my surgery till
eleven, officer. Jackson knows where it is; in the book,
of course. Good morning."

"Thank you, sir. I don't doubt but what you'll be

wanted to give your opinion. Now I'll shut this room up and get in touch with my headquarters at once. Perhaps I should have done so before, but I had to be in here with you, and I don't like using the whistle unless there's something like a scrap on. Good morning, sir."

Having ushered his companions out of the room, the constable closed the door and, having locked it, put the key in his pocket.

"Now, Mr. Jackson," he said, "telephone, please."

"There's one in there, sir," said the butler, pointing to the room they had just left. (The dignity of the Law in action had unconsciously influenced him to adopt a form of address more respectful than that which he had previously used.)

"Yes, I saw that. Receiver off; probably been knocked down. Mustn't touch that," said the constable. "I suppose there's another?"

"Oh, yes, sir. One in the morning-room and another upstairs."

"Right. I'll use the morning-room one. Now, Mr. Jackson, no one's to leave this house till my inspector comes—not even to go into the garden. And, of course, no one's to go into the study."

"No, sir. Certainly, sir. I will see to that at once. Is there anything I can get you, sir?"

The policeman's eyes mellowed.

"We'll talk about that when I've done telephoning, Mr. Jackson," he replied.

"Right, Mr. Raffles," said the butler, his sense of proportion returning to him.

CHAPTER III

INSPECTOR DOBSON TAKES CHARGE

IN spite of the exquisite discretion of Mr. Jackson and the stern restrictive measures imposed by P.C. Raffles—now reinforced by other stalwarts of his own division—a small crowd had collected outside St. Margaret's Lodge by 10 a.m., at which hour a taxicab discharged at the front door Detective Inspector Robert Dobson, of the Criminal Investigation Department, Scotland Yard. A man of normal height and build, normal appearance, normal intellect—normal, in fact, in everything except his powers of observation—Inspector Dobson might have been taken for anything, from a Member of Parliament (twentieth-century style) to a detective (real life). His very normalcy was, after his faculty of observation, his most useful attribute since it enabled him to deal with his fellow-men without setting up those psychological complexes of fear, suspicion, and auto-pseudo-incrimination which the mysterious glances and cryptic utterances of the traditional sleuth must inevitably arouse.

The inspector had brought with him a police surgeon—not because he wanted to, but because routine demanded it. He was convinced that he was himself fully qualified to carry out the superficial medical examination which was all that was possible as long as the body remained where it was. However, the surgeon had got to do it, though the detective was determined to see that the performance interfered to a minimum extent with his own investigations. The two men were met in the hall by the divisional inspector, who rather grudgingly handed over the case to the expert from headquarters ; it was not unnatural that the divisional police should resent the way in which any case to which interest or " kudos " might attach was invariably taken over by Scotland Yard, whilst to them were left the dull and often more dangerous cases which did not catch the public eye. Inspector Dobson was accustomed to the attitude and hardly noticed it. He merely listened to the other's report, making a note of such points as might slip his memory.

" Thank you, Mr. Smithers," he said, when the other had finished, " that sounds quite straightforward. Your constable—Raffles, I think you said his name was—seems to have acted very smartly. What about the relatives, now ? Are they all over the house ? "

" There's the daughter, Miss Emily Smethurst. The butler telephoned to her young man, and he broke the news to her—he's with her now. Took it very pluckily, she did, I must say. No fuss or wanting to interfere in there. I took her in and let her view the corpse, of course——"

" Anyone else go in to view it ? " Inspector Dobson interrupted.

" Only the young man—Mr. Geoffrey Hastings his name is—he's the old man's secretary. Nothing was touched. I can vouch for that ; they stood hand in hand all the time, looking down at it."

The detective nodded.

" That's all there is in the house," Inspector Smithers continued. " I believe there's a sister coming up from the country, but I don't know when she'll get here."

" Right. That'll be all then, I think, Mr. Smithers. You'll be able to leave me a sergeant and two constables for a bit, I dare say. That man Raffles I'd like to have. Thank you. Good morning."

Having thus gently removed the only rival authority, the detective turned to the remaining encumbrance.

" Now then, doctor, we'll have a look at the body. It's been seen by the local man, you'll have heard Inspector Smithers say, and no doubt you'll only want to give it a glance over now. After that I'd like to have it to myself for half an hour and get it photographed, and then it shall be sent to the mortuary and you can do what you like with it."

The divisional surgeon, a fussy and rather pompous little man, did not much relish this thinly veiled dictation from a mere inspector, but he knew enough of the Yard to realize that he was less indispensable to the Chief Commissioner than was the detective, so he swallowed his indignation and followed the other into the study. His examination of the body followed closely on the lines of that made by Dr. Bryant, except that, being a more officious and less busy man than the private practitioner, he took longer over it and talked a good deal more. When it was over, the detective repeated his disentangling act and, heaving a sigh of relief, locked himself into the study and settled down to his examination of the scene of the supposed crime.

His first task was to make a rough plan of the room, which, to save a complicated description, is reproduced on page 21. As will be seen from this, the length of the room ran from the door to the two French windows which faced it. Standing with his back to the door, the inspector marked these two windows, right (R) and left (L). The fireplace, in the wall on his left, was flanked by two leather-covered arm-chairs, by the side of each of which was a small smoker's table. Between the fireplace and the left French window was the writing-table, set at an angle, and in the wall beside it was a small safe. Opposite the fireplace was a large sash window, flanked by bookcases, and in front of this window stood an oak refectory table covered with newspapers and periodicals, mostly of a financial nature. Curtains were still drawn across all the windows, and the electric light was burning.

Having noted these facts, the detective walked over to the body and knelt down beside it. Taking a magnifying glass from his pocket, he closely examined the back of the head, but beyond a slight discoloration of the flesh under the hair at the base of the skull there was no sign of a wound —nothing to indicate the nature of the weapon with which the blow had been dealt. The body, as has been said, was lying face downwards, with the head resting on one crooked arm, whilst the other arm was stretched out at the side. The legs pointed practically to the wall between the two French windows, the head being just past the corner of the writing-table. The face was practically invisible, buried as it was in the coat sleeve, so the detective

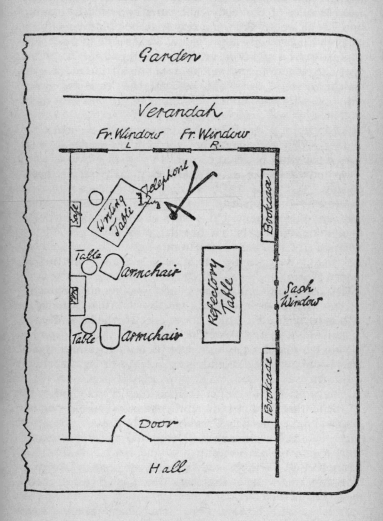

Garden

Verandah

Fr. Window
L.

Fr. Window
R.

Safe

Writing Table

Telephone

Bookcase

Table

Armchair

Refectory Table

Sash Window

Table

Armchair

Bookcase

Door

Hall

21

left it for a moment, turning his attention to the hands and the soles of the feet. The latter appeared to interest him, for he scrutinized them closely through his magnifying glass and rubbed his finger gently on the sole of one. He next turned his attention to the carpet round the body and near the windows, picking up some small pieces of grit which he found on it and placing them carefully in an envelope. Having done this, he rose to his feet and stretched himself.

" Suppose I'd better let them have this body now," he said. " Otherwise they'll be worrying me for it, and I want a couple of hours to myself."

He moved to the door, unlocked it, and put his head outside.

" Jones ! " he called. " Ah, there you are. Bring your things along now, but mind you don't touch anything —anything, mind. Is that ambulance come yet ? "

" Yes, sir ; it's been here ten minutes."

" Right. Just tell the chap we shan't keep him much longer."

He turned back into the room and was presently followed by two men in plain clothes, who set up a heavy camera, with a peculiar adjustable tripod, over the body, and near it standards carrying powerful magnesium light apparatus. Within ten minutes the body had been photographed from several different angles, and the camera men had departed with their traps.

The detective called after them as they left the house :

" Send that stretcher in now. And have those photographs at Superintendent Fraser's room by three. So long."

He then took a piece of chalk from his case and carefully drew a line round the outline of the body, showing the position of all the limbs, the feet, and the head. Two men then appeared with a stretcher, which he directed them to lay beside the body.

" Now then," he said, " give me a hand gently. Just tilt it slowly over on to its back on the stretcher. That's it—gently. Jove! isn't it stiff? Just pull that arm away from the face a minute."

It took the united efforts of two men, one pulling at the arm whilst the other held the body, to move it sufficiently to expose the face. The sight was not a pleasant one; the staring eyes, rimmed, with a suffusion of blood, the half-open mouth, the crusted trickle of blood at the ears combined with the ghastly colour of the skin to produce a gruesome spectacle. The detective, however, appeared quite unmoved. He smelt the lips, opened them further with his fingers, and closely examined the teeth; then once more examined the hands, and particularly the finger-nails. Finally, having emptied the pockets of their contents, he placed the latter, after a brief scrutiny, in a large canvas envelope, sealed it up, and placed it in his despatch case.

"Right you are," he said, "sheet on and take her away. You'll have to be careful getting that arm through the doors."

CHAPTER IV

P.C. RAFFLES SCORES TWICE

HAVING thus disposed of the unfortunate victim of the crime, Inspector Dobson next set to work to examine its setting. He first turned his attention to the windows. The large sash window and the right French window were both curtained, shuttered, and latched; but the left French window, behind the writing-table, though covered by the heavy curtains, had its shutter thrown back and was itself unlatched. Having examined the fastening of the window with great care, Inspector Dobson stepped through it on to the veranda outside, which in turn gave upon the garden. The veranda was stone-paved, and in front of each French window was a doormat. Leaving the garden for future inspection, the detective returned to the room and examined the floor just inside the window. Here again he found a few grains of grit, but it was behind the

23

curtain which covered the right French window that he discovered the largest amount. With a grunt of satisfaction he collected a portion of this, and then turned his attention to the writing-table. On this the first object to catch his eye was the telephone, which, standing on the left-hand side, had evidently been knocked over by the body in its fall, for it lay on its side with the receiver dangling over the edge of the table. Taking an insufflator from his case, the detective blew a cloud of fine powder over both telephone and receiver, but the result was a disappointment, the finger-prints being too blurred to give any useful record.

On the blotter lay a sheet of memorandum paper, with an uncovered fountain pen beside it, but no writing appeared on the paper. Beside it lay a copy of the *Financial News*, with a passage dealing with the artificial silk trade marked in ink. Two drawers of the writing-table were locked ; the remainder appeared to contain principally stationery, bills, and receipts. The leather surface of the table was covered by a good many scratches, most of them old, and a close scrutiny revealed two or three small drops of candle grease which appeared fresh, but there was no candle on the table. An ash-tray contained the stump of a cigar and a cigarette-end, but no other item of interest presented itself.

The safe in the wall beside the writing-table, however, provided Inspector Dobson with plenty of interest, for in the keyhole in the centre rested a bunch of keys. The safe was a heavy one, with a modern combination key and letter lock. If, as seemed likely, the key had been inserted by the intruder, he was evidently unaware of the letter combination, for the safe was still securely fastened. The application of powder in this case brought much more useful information, for the letter lock showed no finger-prints at all.

" Ah, so you worked in gloves, my friend, did you ? " murmured the detective to himself.

Making a mental note that he must find somebody who did know the letter combination in order that he might examine the contents of the safe, Inspector Dobson next turned his attention to the fireplace. This was of the large, open variety, and contained the dead ashes of a fire. An examination of the latter failed to reveal anything of interest, though the detective picked up a couple of cigarette-ends and added them to his collection. In the ash-tray on the smoker's table next the door was the stump of a cigar, and in that next the writing-table two or three cigarette-ends. All these were sealed up in separate envelopes, with a note as to their position. On the right side of the chair which stood between the fireplace and the door, a good deal of cigar ash had fallen on the carpet, but it had been much scattered, possibly by the foot of one of the people who had been in and out of the room, so that it would have been difficult to identify the tobacco from the fine dust which was all that remained. A tray with a decanter of whisky and a half-empty syphon stood on the refectory table, and each smoker's table held a glass smelling of whisky. Both the glasses and the decanter gave excellent impressions of finger-prints, and were carefully set aside by the detective for expert examination.

Having exhausted the possibilities of the study, Inspector Dobson turned his attention to the garden. The veranda outside, as has already been said, was stone paved and yielded no sign of a footprint, but the detective hoped for better things from the grass and gravel paths beyond. To his disappointment, however, he found that, though there had undoubtedly been a heavy dew, the ground, after a spell of dry weather, was still so hard that no impression was made in it by feet—even by the heavy ones of P.C. Raffles, whom he found on guard in the drive. The detective, who had received a favourable impression of this constable from Inspector Smithers' report, condescended to enlighten him as to his disappointment. A slow smile came over the constable's face.

" I think I might be able to help you there, sir," he said. " I didn't like to disturb you while you were in there, but

I think I've found something you'd like to see. If you wouldn't mind stepping this way, sir."

The constable led his superior officer down the drive toward the gate into the street, near which he halted and pointed out a spot in the flower border next the drive where several geraniums had been broken and the earth considerably disturbed.

" By Jove ! " said the detective ; " that's interesting. I wonder what's been happening here.   It doesn't look like digging, and yet why should so many flowers be broken ? May have been an animal got in from the road, of course, but there's nothing to show it. Bother this hard earth, it holds no impressions that are of any use—that looks like a heel mark— ah, and here's another nearer in to the shrubs.   Get hold of the gardener, Raffles.   Perhaps he's been working there."

" I asked him that, sir," replied the constable.   " He says he's not ; and, what's more, that these flowers were all right when he left at five o'clock yesterday evening, because he always looks over them last thing.   Sir John seems to have been very set on his geraniums."

" Good for you, Raffles ! " ejaculated Inspector Dobson. " This is going to be useful, I fancy."

The detective spent twenty minutes in the flower-bed and the shrubbery behind it, but for the time, at any rate, the significance of the discovery appeared elusive, for the traces of the undoubted intruder were too vague to give any indication as to either his identity or his purpose. At last the detective gave it up in disgust, whereupon P.C. Raffles, who had been patiently watching him all this time, while keeping an eye on the gate to guard against an invasion by the curious, again offered his assistance.

" There's one other little thing I think you ought to see, sir," he said.   " If I might get my mate to relieve me on the gate for a bit, I'll show it you—round the back o' the house, it is."

" Certainly," replied the detective.   " I only hope it'll be a bit less disappointing than this one—though this'll fit in somewhere in time, I don't doubt."

The relief was soon effected and the constable led Inspector Dobson round to the back of the house, where most of the offices gave upon a paved yard.

" No footprints on this stuff, I'm afraid, sir," said Raffles ; " but if you'll cast your eye on that scullery window latch . . ."

There was no need to finish his sentence, for the detective was already carefully examining some scratches on the sash just below the latch.

" You'll see the latch itself better from inside, sir," murmured the constable. " The door's just here."

From inside the room it was easy to see deep scratches on the bright imitation brass surface of the latch, suggestive clearly of some metal instrument being used to force it open. The detective was plainly rather excited by the discovery.

" This looks something more like it," he said. Then his face fell. " But, of course, there's nothing to show that it was done last night."

" That's all right, sir," replied P.C. Raffles respectfully. " I asked the butler about that, and he said that latch was only put on yesterday—you'll see it's a new one. The old one had got so weak that it wasn't any use. No doubt when those scratches were made, and that latch was undone when I found it."

" By God, Raffles ! " cried Inspector Dobson ; " you're altogether too smart for a ' pore bloody bobby.' You'll be in an arm-chair at the Yard before you're much older—or, more likely, with a name like yours, you'll be ' last seen swimming into the sunset towards the Island of Capri.' "

P.C. Raffles, who also knew his Hornung, chuckled happily.

CHAPTER V

SOME QUESTIONS

THE scullery door showed no sign of having been tampered with. It had, in fact, been found unlocked in the morning, but as the scullery-maid confessed that, though her orders were to lock it at night, she frequently forgot to do so, there was nothing to show whether the intruder had gone beyond the scullery, even if he had actually entered it. The various passages between the scullery and the study were carefully searched, but yielded no evidence of interest.

"Well," said Inspector Dobson, "I think that's all we can do on this line at the moment. Now I'd like to ask a few questions. Let's see : it was the head-housemaid who found the body, wasn't it ? Send her along to the study, Raffles ; and I'll see the butler after her. Funny thing none of the family showing up ; generally, it takes one all one's time to disentangle oneself from them."

"That's Inspector Smithers, sir," said the constable, loyal to his own chief. "He saw them—Miss Smethurst, that is, and her young man—as soon as he got here, and told them you'd be coming and would let them know when you wanted them."

"So much the better. I can't complain of not having a clear run. Well, send Mary Ann, or whatever her name is, along."

"Alice, sir. Yes, sir," murmured the model lieutenant.

Alice at once disclosed herself to be a treasure—level-headed, methodical and intelligent—but none the less the detective was unable to glean any fresh information from her. She always tidied up the study at about seven in the morning—Sir John would allow none of the under-servants to touch the room. On this occasion she found the door unlocked as usual, but was surprised to find the electric light on. She was crossing the room to draw the curtains and open the French windows, when she saw Sir John's body lying by the writing-table. She knelt down beside it and touched the shoulder, when the stiffness of the body, coupled with the coldness of the hand, at once assured her that her master was dead. She at once went to Mr. Jackson's room and told him the terrible news. The butler was not yet up—the family breakfasted at nine, and it was customary for the master to be called by James, the first footman—he was sitting up in bed drinking his cup of chocolate. He had taken the news very hardly—seemed quite knocked off his balance—but, then, he had been with Sir John a great many years. That was all she had to tell. No, she had not touched anything in the study. She had noticed that the telephone had been knocked over, but nothing else unusual. No, as far as she knew, Sir John never locked the study door.

Alice was succeeded by Mr. Jackson himself. The butler repeated the story of the morning's discovery which he had already told to P.C. Raffles and to Inspector Smithers, not to mention Miss Smethurst, Mr. Hastings, and his fellow-servants. At the end of the recital, Inspector Dobson, who had listened attentively without interrupting, said :

" Thank you, Mr. Jackson ; you've told your story very clearly. Now, I'm going to ask you a few questions, and I want you to take your time and think before you answer them and be quite sure that your answers are correct. A careless answer, which isn't quite accurate, might put me right off the line. Now, in the first place, when did you last see your master alive ? "

The butler paused before replying, but rather because he had been told to than because a pause was necessary.

" Last night, sir, at about two minutes past eleven. Mr. Hastings, Sir John's secretary, had been dining with him and they sat in the study after dinner. Sir John rang for me to let Mr. Hastings out—it's the custom, sir, to ring twice when the butler is only required to let a guest out of the front door—he rang for me at just about a minute before eleven, because I looked at the Room clock at the time. Mrs. Phillips—that's the cook—can confirm that, sir, because she was with me, and I think either she or I made some comment about its being earlier than usual. Mr. Hastings was just coming out of the study when I got into the front hall, but he stopped in the door to talk to Sir John. He—Sir John, that is—was sitting in that arm-chair next the door, smoking, and he asked Mr. Hastings if

29

he'd be in the Row to-morrow morning—that is, of course, this morning (my master had intended to ride himself and had given orders to be called at seven)—but Mr. Hastings said his mare was a bit lame and he didn't think he'd better. Then they just said good night and I let Mr. Hastings out and went to bed."

" Then you didn't return to the study after letting Mr. Hastings out. What do you do about the next day's orders ? "

" I get them when I take the whisky in at ten. If there's anything after that, Sir John rings for me. Yesterday, as a matter of fact, he sent me a message by Mr. Hastings that he would ride in the morning and wanted to be called early."

" Yes ; I was coming to that," said the detective. " I understand from the housemaid that it's the footman's job to call your master. How was it that he didn't tell you that Sir John was not in his bed ? "

" Sir John was to be called at seven, sir, and it was at seven that Alice found him in the study and gave the alarm. As a matter of fact, James must have been a few minutes late, because he was only just coming out of Sir John's bedroom to tell me about his not being there when I came down after being enlightened by Alice."

" I see. What about this chap James ? Has he been with you long ? "

" Not very, sir. About four months, I think. As a matter of fact, I don't know much about him—I didn't engage him myself. Sir John had a way of picking up people and just saying they were coming ; he wasn't a gentleman to argue with. He's quite a good lad, is James. Rather older than the usual run, but there's no harm in that."

The detective made a mental note that it might be worth while to find out a little more about this elderly underling without a past, though there was nothing whatever to connect him with the crime.

" Now, Mr. Jackson," he continued, " about the study windows. Can you tell me whether they were open or shut last night ? "

" Shut, sir, beyond a doubt. I shut them and shuttered them myself at ten last night when I took in the whisky. That was the rule. Sometimes Sir John would open one himself after that—he was fond of fresh air at times. Sometimes he'd smoke his last cigar in the garden before turning in. Then he'd shut it himself when he came in."

" I see," said the detective thoughtfully.

" That may explain how the murderer got in, or it may not. Anyhow, there is no doubt that the window was shut at ten last night ? "

" None at all, sir."

" Well, that's that. Now, about the door. Alice tells me it was unlocked when she went in this morning and that, as far as she knew, Sir John never locked it. So there was no reason why any member of the household should not have gone in after you went to bed ? "

The butler permitted himself a pitying smile.

" I beg your pardon, sir, but there was every reason. It was as much as anyone's place was worth to disturb Sir John in his study of an evening, unless he rang for them. He used to do a lot of his work—his brain work, he used to call it—in there, and after I'd taken in his whisky, or, like last night, after his guest was gone, not even Miss Emily would go in. No, sir, there was no need for Sir John to lock his door."

" I see," said the detective thoughtfully. " But, of course, any outsider who got into the house wouldn't know that he mustn't go in there."

" I beg your pardon, sir ? "

" Nothing. I'd be glad if you'd tell me something about your master. I know, of course, that he was a big financier and all that—that everyone knows—but you can probably give me a look at him that the public doesn't get. Would you say he was a hard man, or a mean man—a man who would be likely to have enemies ? "

This time the butler paused for an appreciable time before answering. At last he said :

" My master *was* a hard man, sir, as the world sees it. To anyone that served him well he was kindness itself, but if he thought anyone wasn't giving him full value, or was trying to take an advantage of him, he wouldn't show him no mercy."

" And that sort makes enemies—and fortunes ? Yes, I suppose so. Now, would you say that Sir John had any particular enemy—anyone who had a special grudge against him ? "

Again the butler thought before replying, but though he racked his brains he was unable to suggest any particular person who might fit this description. Having failed in that direction, the detective started on a fresh tack. He asked the butler whether he had noticed anything different about his master the previous night—any excitement or anxiety ? Jackson replied that he had noticed nothing of the kind.

" Then you would say that there was nothing unusual about the evening ? "

" Nothing, sir," replied the butler. Then, after a pause : " Beg your pardon, sir. Sir John did tell me to get up a bottle of the '96—port, that is, sir. He had done the same the previous Monday. I understood that he was expecting Mr. Hastings might bring him some special news he might want to celebrate."

" No idea what sort of news, I suppose ? "

" Not unless it was about some business deal, sir."

Again the detective could get nothing more definite. Finally, he undid his dispatch-case and laid on the table the articles which he had taken from Sir John's pockets— money, watch, diary, notecase, etc.

" Is that what you'd expect to find in your master's

pockets, Jackson? You must be familiar with what he carried about him."

The butler scrutinized the mournful collection.

" It's all there, sir, that he'd be likely to carry at night. In the day-time he generally carried a memorandum-book as well. I fancy he used it a good deal in his business deals—he had a lot of irons in the fire, and I expect he couldn't carry them all in his head. When he came home, though, he usually locked it up in his writing-table—it was a fairly bulky book."

" Well, it wasn't in his pockets this morning," said the detective, " so it ought to be in the writing-table. Would it be one of these keys? "

He produced from his case the bunch taken from the safe. The butler indicated the appropriate key, and Inspector Dobson opened first one and then the other of the two locked drawers. They contained cheque-books, account-books, correspondence files, and other documents, but the memorandum-book was not there.

" Gone! " ejaculated Inspector Dobson.

CHAPTER VI

EMILY AND ROSAMUND

ON receiving the butler's telephone report of the tragic death of his employer, Geoffrey Hastings, who had been in bed when the call came through, at once hurried on the first clothes he could find, and, though it was only ten minutes' walk, took a taxi round to St. Margaret's Lodge. He was met by Inspector Smithers, of N Division, who tactfully deflected his natural inclination to view the scene of the tragedy and the victim. The inspector told him briefly what had occurred, and repeated the butler's appeal to him to break the news to the dead man's daughter. Hastings, of course, consented, and with a heavy heart took himself upstairs to the first floor, where his fiancée's room was situated. Realizing that the whole domestic staff must by now be throbbing with the news, he judged that to send her maid in with a message asking Emily to see him would inevitably mean the blurting out of the story, probably with gruesome details. He therefore went straight to her door, knocked on it, and in response to an inarticulate murmur, went in.

Emily Smethurst was a good-looking girl of some twenty-five years of age—she herself said that she was for ever and fatally dated by her essentially nineteenth-century name. Without any particularly beautiful features, she was blessed with the lovely complexion that, blooming so astonishingly in the grimy atmosphere of Lancashire, is the essence of all real beauty. Like all Lancashire girls, too, she had her head screwed on very definitely in the right way, and, though capable of passion and even of romance, was incapable of anything resembling hysteria. It was, therefore, no exaggeration on the part of Inspector Smithers when he told his colleague that she had taken the news very pluckily. She was deeply devoted to her father, proud of his success, still more proud of the humble origin from which he had made his way. It was, therefore, no indifference that enabled her to face the shattering blow with apparent calmness, but sheer pluck and self-control.

Inspector Smithers had headed off Geoffrey Hastings from the study because he did not want it disturbed by the coming and going of a countless host, but he naturally would not refuse to allow the dead man's daughter to see her father's body, nor her request that her lover should accompany her. He was a little apprehensive lest she should wish to disturb the position of the body— in his professional eyes a matter of vital importance—but after asking once whether it was quite certain that he was dead and receiving the sad assurance of the doctor's testimony, she made no attempt to touch her father, but stood, hand in hand with Geoffrey Hastings, looking down at the silent form that for so many years had carried the whole of her young love. Her eyes were dim with unshed tears, but the thin line of her lips revealed the still unconscious instinct at the back of her mind—the instinct to pursue relentlessly and punish without remorse the perpetrator of this horrible crime.

She did not stay long in the study, but returned to her room to dress, telling Jackson, as she received his respectful sympathy, to see that Mr. Hastings had some breakfast. Geoffrey was amazed at the calmness and unselfishness which enabled her to think of such a trifle at such a time, but he felt himself quite unable to take advantage of it. Instead, he retired to the morning-room, where smoking was allowed, to light a pipe and think over the bewildering catastrophe that had befallen this family with whose fortunes his own were now so closely welded. Although no less selfish than other men, he was at that moment less concerned with its effect upon his own future than with the problem of how best to help his fiancée to get through the bad time that must inevitably follow with the reaction from the shock. He had the sense to realize that, much as she loved him and loved to have him near her, he could not give her quite the sympathy that another woman could. Her mother, of course, was dead, and her father's sister, apart from the fact that she could not arrive from Devonshire much before the evening, was a century, rather than a generation, older than her niece.

Fortunately there was no great difficulty in finding the right person for the occasion. Emily Smethurst, with countless girl acquaintances of her own age to choose from, had taken for her great friend a woman considerably older than herself, one to whom in this time of trouble she could turn, not only for love and sympathy, but also for the advice which the latter's greater experience and knowledge of the world so well entitled her to give. Rosamund Barretta was at this time barely on the right side of forty, but she was in the full flower of her beauty. Her features and her figure were alike of a classical loveliness, while her complexion, if lacking the youthful freshness of Emily's, yet needed little help from art to complete a radiant picture.

The daughter of a man of good birth but of little else that was good, Rosamund Henderson, when still only seventeen, had met, whilst travelling in Spain with her father, a young Spanish nobleman, who fell instantly in love with her and, to the secret relief of her parent, married her as soon as he could get her admitted to the Church of Rome, and took her to live in the vast but uncomfortable family palace in Madrid. The marriage had been neither a great success nor a notable failure. Count Barretta was, like many men of his race, both romantic and inconstant. He loved his wife passionately at uncertain intervals, reawakening in her each time by his ardour the feelings which he had first inspired. But the intervals of neglect—and they were of increasing length and frequency—were extremely trying. Unfortunately, Barretta's family was as poor as it was ancient. The ancestral palace of Madrid was run by a weird assortment of " retainers " who, probably from sheer laziness, were content to work for their board and lodging alone. But there was little surplus cash with which to provide the beautiful clothes, the entertainments, and the other little luxuries which mean so much in married life. And Rosamund loved beautiful things, beautiful clothes above all else, and it was small consolation to her to have them during the month or two in the year when her husband was making love to her, if for the remainder of the time she had to make them " do " whilst her husband scraped together money to spend on other women.

So, for ten or more years, the marriage had dragged on. Then came the war, and Paul Barretta, as soon as he saw that his country intended to remain neutral, had enlisted in the French Foreign Legion and had been killed. Rosamund returned to England, and in the wave of enthusiasm that passed over the women of the country—partly a desire to serve and partly a fashionable whim—took to nursing in one of the big South London hospitals. Here she met Emily Smethurst, at that time a very junior probationer, who quickly made of the beautiful widow an object for hero-worship. At first it was worship from a distance, but after a time she plucked up courage to invite the adored one to breakfast and a bath at St. Margaret's Lodge. After that the unostentatious luxury of the young probationer's home made her quest of Rosamund's friendship an easy one, and before long the girl's own worth had turned the friendship into a real affection that had grown in the succeeding years into the mutual devotion that now bound them to one another.

Geoffrey's telephone call found Rosamund already up, and within a quarter of an hour a taxi deposited her at the door. As shortly as possible Geoffrey explained to her what had happened, and while they were still talking, the door opened and Emily came into the room. Her face was white and set, but the sight of her friend seemed to break down suddenly the nervous control which her courage had built up to resist the clamouring forces of nature ; her lips trembled, tears rushed into her eyes, and she broke into a fit of weeping so overwhelming that her whole body was shaken by the convulsive sobs. Rosamund ran to her and took her in her arms.

" My darling," she cried. " Don't, Em, darling, don't. I can't bear to hear you cry."

" Oh, Rosa," sobbed the girl ; " how could they ? Who can have done it ? Who can have hated him enough to kill him ? "

" Em, dearest, I hardly know how it has happened, but I am sure it must just have been a burglar who hit him because he was frightened of being caught. No one could have hated him. Everyone loved him."

Rosamund's words, though they bore no weight of reason, were sufficient to restore self-control to Emily. She disengaged herself from her friend's arms, gave herself a shake, and walked over to the mirror to survey the ravages of her emotion.

" Sorry I made such a fool of myself, Rosa," she said. " It has been pretty awful, and I couldn't let go in front of all those policemen and people. Where's Geof? I suppose he tactfully effaced himself when I began. Dear old boy; he's been so splendid—I don't know what I should have done without him. But I *am* glad you've come, darling—it'll make all the difference to have you. Can you stay? Have you had breakfast? Did Geof send for you?"

" Yes. No. Yes," said Rosamund, laughing. " You're rather a wonder, Em; but I know you're right to take it like that. All the same, if you want a good cry, you know where to come for it."

" Thanks, Rosa; I know. But look here, seriously, you must have some breakfast. It's jolly bad to go without your proper meals."

" I quite agree, dear, it is. Of course, you've had yours?"
Emily smiled wanly.

" No, I haven't. I couldn't. But you could and you must. I'll ring and tell Jackson. Omelette?"

" Darling, I'll have some if you will—not otherwise. Even if it's only a cup of coffee and a piece of toast, it'll keep you going till you feel up to something more."

" All right, I'll try," said Emily.

As she moved towards the bell the door of the morning-room opened and Jackson appeared.

" I beg your pardon, miss," he said, " but the Scotland Yard detective would be glad to know if you feel able to see him for a few minutes."

CHAPTER VII

MORE QUESTIONS

INSPECTOR DOBSON bowed to the two ladies.

" I'm sorry to disturb you, miss," he said, addressing Emily, " but there are one or two questions I've got to ask you, and if you can spare me a few minutes now, the sooner I shall be able to clear out and leave you the house to yourself."

" Certainly, Inspector," replied Emily. " Do you mind if my friend, Madame Barretta, stays, or would you rather see me alone ? "

" If you don't mind, miss, that would be best."

Inspector Dobson held the door open for Rosamund, who gave Emily's hand a squeeze and told her that she would wait for her in her sitting-room and have some coffee waiting for her there—the latter a hint to the inspector not to be too long over his interrogation.

" Sit down, Inspector," said Emily, when the door had closed. " I'll tell you anything I can, but I'm afraid I don't know anything at all that will throw any light on this horrible crime."

" Thank you, miss. There's not much I need worry you about now, but I want one or two facts to go on with. In the first place, when did you last see your father alive ? "

" At about seven, or a little later, last night. I was dining with some friends and going to a play and a dance, and I went into his study to say good night to him."

" What time did you return from the dance ? "

" I didn't go to the dance. I felt unwell and came straight home from the theatre—at about half-past eleven, I suppose."

" You didn't go into the study on your return ? "

" No. I never disturb daddy once he's settled down to work after dinner—it was the one thing he couldn't stand. He used to do a lot of his most important work at night. I just went straight up to bed."

" You didn't hear any sound from the study or anywhere else in the house ? "

" No ; nothing at all."

" Neither then nor later ? "

" No."

" Could you see whether the light in the study was on when you went through the hall ? "

" No. I don't think I could have noticed either way. The light in the hall is always on at night, and I suppose that would have stopped the study light from showing under the door, wouldn't it ? "

" Yes, I expect it would, miss," answered the detective. " So you really can say nothing about last night that can help me in any way ? Nothing unusual at all ? "

" Nothing that I noticed, Inspector."

" That's a pity. Your coming in at that time unexpectedly might have made a lot of difference. Still, it can't be helped. Now, about Sir John. I take it he didn't show any signs of expecting anything like this ? "

" What do you mean, Inspector ? I don't understand."

" Only this, miss. A man like Sir John, who has made his way up in life and made his own fortune, is liable to tread on a few people's toes. If he trod a bit hard once or twice he might make some pretty bad enemies. What I mean is, did he ever give you any reason to suppose that he had any bad enemies that might mean him mischief ? "

" No, never ! He didn't talk to me very much about his business. I think he was rather old-fashioned about women and their sphere. I have never had the smallest hint of such a thing."

" Thank you, miss. There was just a chance you might

have heard something. Well, I don't think I need trouble you any more now, miss. I may have to later on, and if you think of anything that might be useful in the meantime, perhaps you'll very kindly let me know."

"Of course I will, Inspector. I'll do anything—*anything*—to help find the fiend that killed my father. You will find him, won't you? If anything is wanted in the way of money you'll let me know, won't you?"

"Thank you, miss; there won't be anything unless it's a reward, but I'll have to consult the Chief about that. Don't you worry, miss, I'm sure we'll get him. Now I want a word with Mr. Hastings; would he be about still, do you suppose, miss?"

"I should think so, Inspector. He was in here when Madame Barretta arrived. I expect he's waiting to see me again. Jackson will find him for you—I'll ring."

"Thank you, miss; please don't trouble; I'll find him. Good morning, miss."

"Good morning, Inspector—and good luck."

Geoffrey Hastings, when he slipped away from the morning-room to leave Emily and Rosamund alone together, had some difficulty in knowing where to turn to continue his own rather harassed meditations. He was in desperate need of a pipe, but neither the drawing-room nor Emily's sitting-room was an eligible setting for man's comforter, and both the morning-room and study were, for their various reasons, out of the question. Eventually he took himself and his Boer tobacco out into the garden, where he paced up and down in a distant corner, the watchful eye of P.C. Raffles keeping him at a sufficient distance to safeguard the precious footprints that he had found. Here Inspector Dobson found him, with his request for an interview.

"Right you are, Inspector," said Geoffrey. "What about out here? I've just got my pipe going, and I'm sure you must be dying for one."

" I am that, sir. But I think we'll go into the study, if you don't mind. There are one or two things in there that I want to ask you. You can smoke in there, of course."

Reluctantly Geoffrey followed him indoors. In spite of the inspector's permission, he knocked out his pipe, probably from a natural feeling that it would be discordant to smoke in a room so lately the scene of tragedy. The detective waved him into the arm-chair which faced the window, the one in which Sir John Smethurst had been sitting when last seen alive—except by the murderer—and himself sank into the companion chair on the opposite side of the fireplace.

" Now, Mr. Hastings," he said, " I want to hear, in the first place, all about last night. Tell it in your own way and I'll try not to interrupt. I'll ask you questions about it afterwards."

" All right, Inspector," replied Geoffrey. " I don't know that there's much to tell, but here goes. I arrived here at about ten minutes to eight; dinner was at eight, but the old man was such a stickler for punctuality that I was always in a funk of being late, and used to put my watch seven minutes fast to be on the safe side. We had dinner alone together and talked about ordinary things—politics and so on; he never would spoil his meals with business. After dinner we got down to it. He went through a variety of things—you know he had a lot of irons in the fire—and I made some notes of things he wanted done. Show 'em you if you like. We spent a good deal of time over artificial silk—he was thinking of taking it up. I think we were talking about that when Jackson brought the whisky in at ten, as usual, and got his orders. We went on talking shop till about a quarter to eleven, and then we just sat in these chairs for a bit and drank a whisky and smoked a cigar. I think I had a cigarette. We talked about riding—Sir John was one of the liver brigade. He told me to tell Jackson that he'd ride in the morning—he doesn't like being disturbed in here ; he wanted to be called early—seven, I think it was. Then at eleven he shot me out—said he wanted to work. So I just said good night and went. Jackson let me out. I had a word or two with him, got a taxi outside, and drove to my Club. That's all I know —unless you want any more about me ? "

" May as well have it, Mr. Hastings. I shall have to ask everybody that sort of thing as a matter of form."

" Righto. As I said, I got a taxi in the Blenheim Road and drove to the Club—the Blue Stocking, in Pall Mall. I played bridge there till about one and then cleared out. I had a bit of a head from smoking too much, or something of the kind, so I strolled down through Trafalgar Square to the Embankment, sat there a bit, and then walked back home. I live close here, you know—big block of flats in St. John's Road. Don't know what time I got in—somewhere getting on for three, I suppose. Went to bed and slept pretty sound till Jackson rang me up and told me about this damn business. Rest you know."

The detective had jotted down notes of the other's account as he went along. He now read them out to Geoffrey and asked him to confirm their accuracy.

" Thank you, Mr. Hastings," he said, when it was done. " It's as well to get one's first impressions quite accurate. A mistaken primary impression may upset one's whole apple-cart. Now for some questions. First of all on your account. Was there anything special about your dining with Sir John last night ? Did he ask you for some particular reason ? Was there any fixed day in the week for you to dine with him, or anything of that kind ? "

" Oh, no," said Geoffrey. " I often dined with him, either to talk business or just for my blue eyes. You know, of course, that I'm engaged to Miss Smethurst—that was one reason for my dining here fairly often. Last night, as it happened, she was going out with some friends, so he asked me because he said he would be lonely."

43

" I see. No special reason. And there was nothing out of the ordinary about the business you were discussing last night ? "

" No ; only what I've told you. Artificial silk was the principal thing, but it was all more or less routine."

" And you noticed nothing out of the ordinary about Sir John ? Nothing that could possibly point to an expectation or fear of anything happening ? "

" Nothing whatever."

" No ; it wasn't likely that there would be anything. Well, I don't think I need bother you at the moment about your own movements, they're not likely to have any bearing on it. Now I am going to ask you one or two questions that I want you to think very carefully about before answering—their importance lies only in their accuracy of detail. In the first place, you said you both smoked last night. Now, I want you to tell me, if you can, what you each smoked and what you did with your cigar or cigarette ends."

Geoffrey stared.

" Good Lord, Inspector," he said, " that's asking rather a lot. I know I smoked one or two cigarettes while we were talking business—I think I chucked them in the fire. And I smoked probably a couple more afterwards when we were drinking our whisky—they would either be in the fireplace or in that ash-tray. Sir John smoked one cigar directly after dinner and while we were talking business. I think he stubbed it out in that ash-tray on the writing-table. He started another when we sat down in the arm-chairs afterwards—I think he was still smoking it when I left. That's all I can remember."

" Thank you, Mr. Hastings. That's very clear and it may be helpful—one never knows. Now, about this safe. The key was found in the lock, but the door was not unlocked. Either Sir John had himself been using the safe and forgot to take out the key, or else the murderer tried to open the safe and failed because he didn't know the combination. Had you any reason to suppose that Sir John was going to use the safe last night?"

"None."

"Would anyone else know the combination besides Sir John?"

"I know," replied Geoffrey. "He told me in case anything happened to him. I don't believe anybody else knows it."

"I'm glad to hear you know it, sir. I want to see inside that safe. Will you kindly open the safe for me—here are Sir John's keys. You'd better let me know the word."

"The word is 'Fidelity.'" Geoffrey took the keys, arranged the combination letters and turned the lock. The door swung open. "There you are, Inspector."

Inspector Dobson bent down and eagerly scanned the interior of the safe. There were two shelves. One was empty, the other held ledgers and note-books. Below were two small steel drawers, one holding a bag of golden sovereigns and two bags of silver, the other banknotes to the value of nearly fifteen hundred pounds. The inspector whistled.

"By Jove!" he said, "that's a lot of money to keep about you. Was it known that there was so much cash in this safe?"

"Not generally, I don't suppose," replied Geoffrey. "I knew he kept a good deal there. He kept a large sum on deposit at the bank as well. He said it was a golden maxim for a man who dealt in big money to be able to put his hand on it at a moment's notice. He made no attempt to conceal it as far as I know. It might have been known in the house that there was a large sum there."

"In the house? The servants, you mean?"

"Possibly."

The detective nodded slowly.

"Interesting," he said.

CHAPTER VIII

A CALL IN THE NIGHT

GEOFFREY was able to reinforce the butler's statement about the windows being shut ; they were shut when he went at eleven. He was, however, unable to throw any light on the missing memorandum-book. It might, he thought, be in Sir John's desk at the office. He knew Sir John generally had it about him, but he doubted whether it was so closely guarded a treasure as Jackson had led the detective to suppose. After getting the address of the office, Inspector Dobson said he would like to have a word with James, the footman.

" Perhaps, sir," he added with a twinkle, " James might kill two birds with one stone by bringing us a glass of something ? I expect you could do with it after all this business—I know I could."

" My dear Inspector, I'm sorry," cried Geoffrey, jumping up and touching the bell. " I ought ·to have thought of it—it's a first-rate idea. Oh, Jackson," he said, as the butler appeared, " the inspector wants to have a word with James. Send him up, will you, and tell him to bring the whisky and two glasses."

James and the glasses were not long in appearing.

" Don't go, James," said Geoffrey ; " the inspector wants a word with you. Say when, Inspector. There you are. Good luck to you—and to your quest. Well, if you've done with me, I must be off to the office. You know where to get me if you want me."

Geoffrey was not sorry to get away from the atmosphere of inquisition, easy as the inspector had made it for him. He found Emily and Rosamund together in the former's sitting-room, but he did not stay long with them, as it was essential that he should take hold of the strings at the office ; the death of a big financier was apt to have repercussions outside his family circle.

Meanwhile, Inspector Dobson was having a good look at " James, the footman." He confined his questions to the calling of Sir John that morning, his only object at the moment being to discover whether the footman was the sort of man whose past might be worth looking into. He arrived at no very clear decision on the point, but the interview had not been without its use, and as he got his insufflator to work on the silver salver and the whisky decanter he congratulated himself on the neatness of the trick by which he had got impressions of two sets of finger-prints without either Geoffrey Hastings or James being aware of it.

The detective was packing up his various " exhibits " preparatory to departure when the butler appeared and announced that a man from the Telephone Service had called to see whether the telephone in the study was out of order, as the exchange had been unable to get any reply from it.

" My God ! " said the detective : " I'd forgotten all about that damn 'phone. What a bit of luck I hadn't gone. Show him up, Jackson ; I'll see him about it."

The butler soon reappeared with the telephone mechanic.

" Don't go, Jackson," said the detective ; " I may want you about this. You're from the Telephone Service, are you, young fellow ? Show me your card. I'm Detective-Inspector Dobson, of the C.I.D. Right, that's in order. Now, then, what about this telephone ? "

" I was told to come round and see if it had gone ' dis,' sir. Exchange say they've been trying to get a call through for hours, and can't get an answer."

" Well, that's not to be wondered at," said the detective. " If you look at it, you'll see why exchange can't get an answer. It's been knocked down. No, don't touch it. It'll do as it is for a bit. But look here, Jackson, you've been using another telephone in the house. This must be only an extension; how is it that the exchange say they can't get an answer ? "

" This isn't an extension, sir," replied the butler ; " this is a separate line. There's a 'phone in the morning-room and an extension in Miss Emily's sitting-room, but Sir John would have a separate line for this room. I fancy he didn't want the possibility of listening-in on his conversations. You see, sir, as I told you, Sir John did a lot of his biggest work in here. He'd have long-distance calls through all over the place—Liverpool, Manchester, and so on, let alone London. No, sir, it wouldn't have done for Sir John to be on an extension."

" I see. No, I suppose it wouldn't. Well, young fellow ; I don't think you need wait ; you can tell your people that there was a murder here last night and the 'phone was knocked over. I'll put it right again later. Here, hold hard a minute." The inspector was evidently excited by an idea that had occurred to him. " If that 'phone was knocked over, and the earpiece came off the hook like that, wouldn't it have put a call through to the exchange ? "

" It would that, sir," replied the mechanic.

" Would the exchange have a note of the time ? "

" I doubt it, sir. You see, a good many calls come through. They might, of course, if it was a slack time. I don't know much about exchange work myself, I'm out on the lines all the time."

" It's worth trying," said the inspector. " Here, Jackson, where's that other 'phone ? "

" In the morning-room, sir, just across the hall."

The detective hustled them out of the study and, locking the door, went straight to the telephone in the morning-room.

A CALL IN THE NIGHT

" Supervisor'll be able to tell me, I suppose? What's the number of Sir John's line? Regent 5505? Hullo. Hullo, Exchange. I want Supervisor, please, *Supervisor!*" A pause. " Hullo, is that Supervisor? This is Detective-Inspector Dobson, of the Criminal Investigation Department, Scotland Yard. Your people have just sent a man round to inquire about a number—Regent 5505—that's been ' dis ' for some time. As a matter of fact, there was a murder here last night, and the telephone was knocked over. Now, I take it that when the 'phone was knocked over, a call would have been put through. I want to know if the time of that call was noted. Can I speak to the operator? "

" The night operator's off duty now," came the voice of the Supervisor ; " but, as a matter of fact, he reported the occurrence before he went off. It seems it was a quiet time and Regent 5505 put a call through, but when the operator asked for the number there was no reply. He rang through more than once, but still there was no reply, so he gave it up. A call was put through from a City number to Regent 5505 this morning, and as there was still no reply we sent a linesman round."

" Yes, but the call in the night," cried the detective ; " did the operator note the time of it ? "

" Not exactly when it was made," came the reply ; " but when he couldn't get a reply he seems to have noted the time—11.50 p.m. it was then. Probably that was about five minutes after the call came through."

" 11.45 p.m. ! " cried Inspector Dobson. " Then that must be the time the murder was committed ! "

CHAPTER IX

MR. SAMUEL McCORQUODALE

IN spite of the fact that the early—tipsters'—editions of the evening papers contained no reference to Sir John Smethurst's death, the news had reached the City over the tape, so that when Geoffrey Hastings arrived at his office he found it in a state of great consternation and confusion. He was greeted with considerable relief by the chief clerk, Mr. Morrison, who had felt himself quite unable to cope with the problems which he saw looming up in the immediate future. James Morrison had been in Sir John Smethurst's service for ten years, knew all the intricacies of his various undertakings—or thought he did—and received a salary which suggested a post of much greater importance than that which he actually held. But he was essentially a clerk, and he could not face responsibility. He was a mine of financial knowledge and could do anything he was told, but initiative was beyond him. Therefore he welcomed the arrival of Hastings, a man of far inferior knowledge and experience than himself and of whom he was accustomed to speak with some disparagement, but one who, with a Public School training and wide general experience, possessed in a crisis exactly the qualification which he himself lacked.

Geoffrey, in fact, thought Morrison unnecessarily flustered by the catastrophe. It was natural that he should be worried and distressed, but the head-clerk appeared quite bewildered and so jumpy that he was of very little use in tackling the business that must be undertaken without delay. Sending him back to his own room, Geoffrey sent telegrams to Sir John's two executors, both old Lancashire friends, and then settled down to deal with the correspondence which was awaiting the dead man's consideration.

A large amount of it could be dealt with by an obvious formula : " In view of the sudden death of Sir John Smethurst, consideration of this matter must be postponed until his executors, etc." Some of the morning's correspondence was of a type which he normally dealt with himself, but there were one or two matters which should have been dealt with by Sir John and which so clearly required an immediate and definite answer that Geoffrey felt he must take upon himself the responsibility of settling them without delay. He set to work to grapple with this task, but found himself constantly interrupted by telephone and personal calls, nearly all connected with the startling catastrophe that must have brought dismay into many business houses in the City. The telephone calls he was able to dispose of with a few words, but the personal visits were a different matter. Some of the callers were men of importance and could not be curtly turned away ; others were of no importance and could be and were. One of the latter was a particularly bright example of the less pleasant elements in the world of finance ; he was the proprietor of a bucket-shop of doubtful character, and his business, baldly put, was to offer the dead man's secretary a sum of money in return for " stable information " as to the probable future of his late employer's holdings.

The toes of Geoffrey's right foot had barely ceased to tingle when a visitor of a very different type was announced. Mr. Samuel McCorquodale was one of the four or five men in the financial world who had competed on more or less equal terms with Sir John Smethurst—equal, that is to say, in wealth and ability, though not in experience or prestige, for McCorquodale was still in the forties, and his reputation was not nearly such a clean one as Sir John's. What he lacked in experience, however, he nearly made good by a really remarkable " flair," and the advantage a character for straight dealing gave to Smethurst was counter-balanced by the greater freedom of action which McCorquodale enjoyed from his complete lack of scruple.

Geoffrey Hastings disliked Mr. McCorquodale more than a little and for more reasons than one. In the first place, his name was Samuel, and in the second his name was McCorquodale, and Geoffrey, who loved Scotland as much as he hated Palestine, was infuriated by the unnatural union. This was mere prejudice ; a more legitimate cause for dislike was the " freedom of action " which has already been referred to. But beneath all this lay the real reason, which was that Mr. Samuel McCorquodale had had the audacity to harbour aspirations to the hand of his rival's fair daughter, and had not had the decency to cancel those aspirations in full upon the announcement of its capture by Mr. Geoffrey Hastings. In other words, McCorquodale had made love to Emily Smethurst and, in spite of her engagement, was still doing so. This may be conceded as a legitimate grievance, and one can hardly be surprised that Geoffrey's toes began to tingle afresh when the name of Mr. Samuel McCorquodale was announced.

It can be imagined, therefore, with what surprise Geoffrey heard the object of his rival's call. Without beating about the bush, McCorquodale asked Geoffrey to come to him as his secretary.

" Don't know what Smethurst gave you," he said, " but I suppose it was round about six or seven hundred. I'll give you a thousand, and I'll tell you straight why I want you. You know the ropes, of course—so do others that I could get for half that. But you know what others don't, and that is what Smethurst was up to. We've spent a good deal of time and money fighting each other, and now he's out of the way I expect to pick up one or two things that I might otherwise have missed. That's where you'll be worth money to me; you know where he's had the pull of me and you can get it for me now. Yorkshire Petroleum, for instance, and that Rio Electrification concession. I'd be prepared to do something on a commission basis if that attracted you. Anyhow, I want you and I'm not afraid to let you know it—that's my way, and it's a way that's not let me down yet. Think it over and let me know to-morrow. May seem a bit quick before the old man's under ground, but if you come I want you at once. No, don't bother to pull out any talk now. Think it over. Take one? 'Morning."

Geoffrey sat back in his chair and watched the back of Mr. Samuel McCorquodale depart, unhastened, through the door. His first thought was amazement at the colossal nerve of the man, but as that subsided he saw the point of McCorquodale's remarks. Quite obviously his knowledge of Smethurst's transactions and methods would be of immense value to Smethurst's late competitor. Then he began to boil up again, this time with indignation at the blatant indecency of the man's approach to himself; quite evidently financial considerations were all that appealed to Mr. McCorquodale, and he judged others by a like standard. But Geoffrey had to admit that, granted that standard, the man had approached him fairly and had made him a straight and generous offer. Finally, though he loathed the man and hated the idea of transferring his service to such a master, he could not fail to recognize that this was an opportunity which only came once in a lifetime. It would mean the immediate possibility of marriage to Emily Smethurst on his own standing, and not on whatever she might bring to the match. To a proud man, that was a consideration that outweighed a good deal of personal inclination.

For half an hour Geoffrey sat turning the matter over in his mind, at one moment rejecting the idea with righteous obloquy and suitable addresses, the next feeling his determination weaken before the insidious appeal of interest. Finally, like a wise man he decided to lay the problem before his wife-to-be and leave her to settle it. He was already beginning to attach considerable value to the unreasoning, and sometimes unreasonable, feminine instinct which is so often and so aggravatingly right.

Having arrived at this decision he put the matter out of his mind and returned to the work in which he had been interrupted. In spite of further interruptions, he had got through the bulk of it by three o'clock, by which time he had begun to realize that he had had neither breakfast nor lunch. As the executors would probably arrive at about four and would be likely to get straight to business and keep at it till late, Geoffrey decided to go out now and get a scratch meal while he could. He was just leaving the lift with his laudable object in view when he bumped into the now familiar figure of Inspector Dobson.

" Hullo, Inspector," he said. " More conundrums for me ? "

" Not at the moment, sir," replied the detective. " I just want to have a look for that memorandum-book, and perhaps have a word or two with your chief clerk, if I may."

" Right you are, Inspector," said Geoffrey. " I'd better come with you if you're going to ransack the old man's room ; I'm responsible for it till the executors take over."

" You are welcome to come, sir," replied the inspector, " but I think you should realize that you have no power to prevent me ransacking—as you call it—wherever I like, provided I produce a search warrant."

Geoffrey laughed.

" I know, Inspector," he said ; " I was only chaffing. Of course, you're the ' god in the machine ' in this show. Here we are. You've got the keys, I suppose."

The inspector produced Sir John's bunch and Geoffrey pointed out the one that would fit the desk. The inspector searched the two or three locked drawers but found neither the memorandum-book for which he was looking, nor anything else that appeared to bear on the case, though he asked to be allowed to take a copy of a list of Sir John's holdings. As he finished locking the last drawer, he turned to Geoffrey and said :

" May I have a look at your keys a minute, Mr. Hastings ? "

Geoffrey was considerably taken aback by this abrupt demand, and for a second he hesitated to comply with it, but, realizing that no good would come of antagonizing the Scotland Yard man, he handed over his bunch of keys without speaking.

The detective had singled out from Sir John's bunch the keys of the writing-table at St. Margaret's Lodge and of the desk in the office. He now carefully compared these with Geoffrey's bunch, and then handed the latter back to its owner.

" Thank you, sir," he said. " I just wanted to know if there were any duplicates about. Nobody else is likely to have one, I suppose ? "

" Not that I know of," Geoffrey replied.

" Probably there aren't any. Now, may I have a word with the head clerk here ? Just a matter of form—I needn't keep you."

Having introduced Morrison to the detective, Geoffrey hurried out again to his belated meal. This time he safely escaped from the building, but there was a frown on his face and he muttered to himself :

" Now, what's that chap after ? Is he squinting down his nose at me ? "

Up in the office Inspector Dobson, as he waved Morrison to a chair, was saying to himself :

" No, my young friend, you've got no duplicate keys, but I'll want to know whether you really were at your club between eleven and one last night, all the same."

CHAPTER X

SCOTLAND YARD THINKS IT OVER

AFTER spending half an hour in trying to fathom the perturbation of Mr. James Morrison, Inspector Dobson came to the conclusion that the time had arrived when he should report his investigations on the case to his superior officer. He therefore took the Underground from the Mansion House to Westminster, and five minutes later was in his chief's room at Scotland Yard.

Superintendent Fraser was an officer of very different type from his lieutenant. The word " normal " could be applied neither to his brain nor to his body. He owed his present position more to the former than to the latter, though, during his active days, his powerful frame had carried him successfully through many an ugly situation. Now that his work was necessarily of a sedentary character the great muscles had largely turned to fat and his figure had become enormous—he was irreverently referred to among his colleagues as " the Super-abundant." Owing to this handicap, he did not as a rule attempt to take an active part in the various investigations for which he was responsible, but gave all his attention to the consideration of the facts collected for him by his subordinates. To this work he was able to bring an intellect of quite exceptional capacity, combining a clear and logical reasoning faculty with imagination and a sixth sense of intuition which can sometimes get round a brick wall which logic and reason can only kick against.

The superintendent greeted the inspector with a nod.

" Morning, Dobson," he said. " Smethurst case, isn't it ? " He drew a paper wrapper towards him and glanced at the single sheet of foolscap that was all that, at the moment, it contained. " Born Haslingden, Lancs, '65. Cotton spinner, lad to department foreman. Chucked his job suddenly in '91 and left Lancashire. Believed to have been in United States and South America. Returned '96 with money and a wife. Bought a spinning machinery business, sold it, two or three other undertakings, and filed his petition in bankruptcy 1900. Some suspicion of fraud, not proceeded with. Made a fortune in rubber boom 1908. Since then has gradually established himself as one of the half-dozen biggest men in finance. Believed to have lost heavily in Russian holdings, owing to the war and revolution, and also over fall of German mark, but position still apparently substantially unshaken. Personal and business reputation high. Nothing known against him other than above suspicion at time of bankruptcy. That's all I know, Dobson, except what we all know. Now you talk."

Inspector Dobson talked for an hour and a half, laying before his chief the story of the tragedy as it had unfolded itself to him, and continuing with an account of his own investigations. Superintendent Fraser sat with his eyes shut throughout the whole recital, with an untouched sheet of foolscap before him. Twice only did he interrupt the inspector's narrative. First, when Dobson referred to the grit behind the curtain of the right front window, he asked for an estimate of the quantity. On hearing that it amounted to approximately the contents of a teaspoon he raised his eyebrows, but made no comment. Secondly, at the reference to candle grease on the writing-table, he asked if there was any sealing wax on the table or in the drawers, and told the inspector, who could not give a positive answer, to make inquiries on the point.

" Now, Dobson," said the superintendent, " we'll just see if the post-mortem report is ready ; then we can make a summary."

" I doubt if it will be, sir," replied the inspector. " I met Dr. Blathermore as I was coming in, and he was only then going in to start it. Said he'd had to go out on another case soon after he got started on it this morning."

" Well, he's had two hours on it—he ought to have come to some general conclusion, anyhow. We'll go down to the P.M. room—he won't like being interrupted and it would make him sicker than ever if we asked him to come up here." The superintendent rose ponderously from his chair. " By the way," he added, " you didn't say anything to him about the time of that telephone call ? "

" I'm afraid I did tell him that, sir," replied the inspector. " He asked me if anything fresh had turned up and I just mentioned that, as it was a salient point."

" Shouldn't have. Might suggest time of death to him —his job to find out for himself. Never mind, can't be helped. Come on."

The two officers made their way through a labyrinth of passages to the mortuary and its adjoining post-mortem room. They found Dr. Blathermore in the latter, busily engaged upon his gruesome task. The body was lying face downwards, covered by a waterproof sheet up to the shoulders, and the surgeon, with a magnifying glass in one hand and a probe in the other, was poring over a gaping wound at the back of the head. He was so engrossed that he did not notice the arrival of his visitors until Superintendent Fraser spoke.

" Sorry to interrupt you, doctor," he said. " We're just making a summary of this case. Glad if you could let us know what you make of it—far as you've got." The superintendent never wasted words.

" Ah, Superintendent, is that you ? " said the surgeon, looking up. " That is not without interest." He tapped the dead man's shoulder with his magnifying glass. " This injury "—pointing to the head—" is terrific. The base of the skull is crushed like an eggshell. I should say a blow of great force was dealt, and with an instrument of considerable weight—concentrated weight. That is to say, something more like a heavy hammer or a burglar's ' life-preserver,' rather than a poker or a heavy stick."

" Ah, yes, Inspector," interrupted the superintendent, turning to Dobson, " I meant to ask you. What about the weapon ? Anything in the room ? Poker ? War trophy ? "

" No, sir ; nothing I should consider suitable. The poker was only a bayonet—a long thin one—French, I should fancy. I couldn't see anything heavy enough to do that. I looked at this wound myself, sir, and formed the opinion which Dr. Blathermore has given, that the blow was terrific."

The surgeon sniffed. Just like a detective, he thought, to pretend that he knew something about doctoring.

" Then you've no doubt about the cause of death ? " inquired the superintendent. " No contributory cause ? Nothing in the stomach, I suppose ? "

" The organs are in the pathological laboratory. Dr. Jeacocks is going over them. I do not anticipate any result other than negative," replied the surgeon.

" No, hardly necessary. ' Anyhow, the man is dead, whether stone or lump of lead.' " The superintendent's companions stared at him. " All right. Only Gilbert. Now, what about time of death. Tell us anything about that ? "

The surgeon drew himself up.

" I have formed an opinion. I must say that we are not helped in these matters by the delay which always seems to occur before the surgeon has an opportunity of examining the body. I understand that the death was reported soon after seven o'clock this morning, but I did not see the body till ten, and then only a superficial examination was possible." The surgeon was taking this Heaven-sent opportunity to air a grievance. " Subsequently, I did not receive the body for a further two hours. Unfortunately, after that I was called away upon another case, so that it was after four before I was able to start any detailed examination. That sort of thing does not render one's work any easier."

The superintendent waited in silence for this tirade to finish ; then, without commenting on it, said :

"And your opinion, doctor ? "

" The opinion I formed at my first examination was that death had occurred nearly twelve hours previously. My subsequent detailed examination suggests a rather shorter period. I put the time of death at about 11.30 to 12 p.m. Half an hour on either side would not be beyond the bounds of possibility."

" Thank you, doctor," said the superintendent. " That's the sort of thing we want to go on with. Won't bother you any more now. Get your full report later, no doubt. Good night."

Outside in the passage the superintendent turned to his subordinate.

" Don't know that I quite trust that little man's judgment," he said. " Bit too full of his own importance, and too cocksure. Wish you hadn't mentioned that time to him. Still, if that's right, his opinion doesn't matter."

Back in his office, Superintendent Fraser lowered himself softly into his capacious chair and drew a sheet of foolscap towards him.

" Now, Dobson," he said, " let's get some of it on paper."

For nearly two hours more the pair sat, thrashing out the details of the case, separating the essential from the unessential. At the end of the time the paper before Superintendent Fraser was covered with his handwriting, a fine neat caligraphy, quite out of keeping with his appearance. It read as follows :

1. *Time of Murder :*
   (*a*) Telephone call 11.45. Very suggestive, but not entirely reliable.

(b) Medical report gives limits 11–12.30, probably 11.30–12. May have been suggested by knowledge of telephone call.

(c) In any case 11 is the limit, as S. was seen alive at that hour.

2. *Access to Room :*
   (a) By door in hall by someone resident in house.
   (b) By door in hall by someone who entered through scullery window.
   (c) By French window, probably when S. was strolling in garden. This is supported by presence of gravel grit on S.'s shoes and on carpet and behind curtains, but amount in latter case seems excessive and suggests possibility of fake.

3. *Motive :*
No evidence yet. Examine will.

4. *Prominent Persons :*
   (a) *Emily Smethurst* (25), daughter. Evidently devoted.
   (b) *Geoffrey Hastings* (35), secretary and prospective son-in-law. Knew of contents of safe, but also knew letter-combination, which was not used. States left house 11 p.m. (confirmed by butler) drove to Blue Stocking Club (find taxi-driver), played bridge till 1 a.m. (check), then walked to Embankment and home to St. John's Road (looks fishy, but time is well beyond limit fixed by medical report). Nothing known against ; inquire further.
   (c) *Henry Jackson* (65), butler. Served twenty-three years. Apparently too old to strike such a violent blow. Character excellent. Appeared unduly distressed by news of S.'s death.

(*d*) *James Riley* (32), footman. Engaged by S., apparently
without character, four months before murder.
Born in Oldham, Lancs. States served with S.'s
son, killed in war. Since then odd jobs till S.
picked him up. Trace.

(*e*) *James Morrison* (53), chief clerk to S. for ten years.
In highly nervous condition when interviewed, but
apparently weak and nervous type.

5. *Points to follow up* :

(*a*) Weapon. Search neighbourhood.

(*b*) Memorandum-book. Search St. Margaret's Lodge
and City office.

(*c*) Will. Examine.

(*d*) Candle grease on writing-table. Why ?

(*e*) Cigars and cigarettes. Two cigars smoked by S.
Why does one (on smoker's table) smell strongly
of whisky and other not ? Why, also, was former
only half smoked ? Five Philip Morris cigarettes,
probably smoked by Hastings, in fireplace and
ash-tray on smoker's table ; one cigarette with
unknown Turkish hieroglyphic in ash-tray on
writing-table, smoked by whom ?

(*f*) Who lay in geranium-bed and opened scullery window ? Anyone seen loitering about in neighbourhood ?

(*g*) S.'s financial affairs. Look into principal undertakings. May be acute rivalry or other trouble.

" There you are, Dobson," said the superintendent ;
" that'll do to go on with. Now, you go off home and
have a good supper and smoke a pipe with that in front
of you. You'll probably think of something else. First
thing to-morrow, get hold of that will—may point somewhere. Get up to the Lodge some time and just go through
that killing act from behind the curtain with somebody—

I'm not quite happy about that. And I want to know a lot more about this chap Hastings—got a big stake in Smethurst's affairs—may be all right, may not. Particularly, check every minute of his time from leaving the Lodge at 11 p.m. up to, say, 12.30 or 1 a.m. Never be satisfied with an alibi unless it's doubly or trebly checked. 'Night."

When the detective had gone, Superintendent Fraser leant back in his chair for some time, his eyes closed, and his fingers playing with his pencil. Presently, as if unconsciously, the pencil began to form letters on the paper on his desk. The superintendent sat up and saw the paper before him. On it was scrawled "HASTINGS." The superintendent stared at it, then drew it towards him and added the following words :

" Why did he not tell Dobson that Smethurst got up a special bottle of port for him last night and on the previous Monday ? "

CHAPTER XI

" CHERCHEZ LA FEMME "

INSPECTOR DOBSON rose the next morning like a giant refreshed. He had followed the superintendent's advice overnight, and had smoked several pipes while he turned over the events of the day in his mind, with the result that he was able to form a definite plan of campaign to follow next day. Then he had put the case out of his mind, and spent an hour before going to bed extracting harmony from a flute, while Mrs. Dobson sat patiently by occasionally murmuring some piece of gossip about Tooting society. The detective's brain was thus able to quiet down before sleep had to be courted and that, with the assistance of the finest hot-water bottle in the world, made sleep easy to win.

The inspector, therefore, woke refreshed and with a zest for the work before him. Ham and eggs, accompanied by an old-fashioned pint of mild beer, another pipe, a glance at the *Mail*, and he was ready to start on his quest. His first move was an Underground journey to St. John's Wood. He was greeted respectfully by Jackson, who informed him that Miss Smethurst had just gone out, in company with Madame Barretta, who had called for her directly after breakfast, but that Mrs. Spurling, Mr. Smethurst's sister, was in and had expressed a wish to see the detective if he came. Dobson decided that he had better get his interview with the lady over at once, though he expected to learn nothing of interest.

Mrs. Spurling was the widow of a country clergyman, and had been living for some years in her late husband's parish upon a comfortable income supplied by her brother. Probably life at Dumbleton-cum-Bumble was not over full of thrills, for the lady, beneath a decent cloak of melancholy, was quite evidently seething with excitement at being so closely connected with a *cause célèbre*. Her desire to see the detective arose clearly from a thirst for inside information, though she was quite ready to talk herself, at the inspector's request, about her late brother. Her narrative appeared unlikely to throw any light upon the problem until, as an afterthought, she remarked that there was one thing which she knew and which she thought was not generally known, though she didn't see what it could have to do with this sad occurrence, and she didn't know that she ought to say anything about it. The detective applied the few words of pressure that were evidently expected, whereupon Mrs. Spurling said :

" I believe there was some woman in my brother's life. Of course, he was married, but I don't mean that, nor dear Emily. I mean a Woman. I never heard him mention anyone in that way, and of course he wouldn't, and I'm sure dear Emily knew nothing about it ; but one day when he was staying with me at Dumbleton—he used to come every year, you know, at Whitsun, as regular as clockwork— one day I picked up a cigarette-case that was lying in an armchair in which he had been sitting, and as I picked it up it came open in my hand—quite by accident, you know —and there inside, opposite the cigarettes, was the photograph of a Woman. I suppose she was beautiful, but it wasn't a face I could care for at all—too bold, and big dark eyes that didn't look quite nice. Of course, I shut the case up and put it back where I had found it, but I didn't feel at all happy, and I quite blushed when I saw my brother next. It was a great shock to me, I can assure you."

Inspector Dobson tried his best to look shocked also.

" That's an interesting point, madam," he said. " There was no name on the photo, I suppose—on the back, perhaps ? "

" Oh, I didn't look at the back." The good lady was further shocked. " I shouldn't dream of prying. No ; there was no name, and I don't know who she could have been."

" And, of course, you've never met her in the flesh ? "

" Oh no ! " Mention of the word " flesh " seemed to bring fresh embarrassment. " Oh no. I'm sure I've never met her. I don't often come to London, you know, so I shouldn't have been likely to meet her, even if she ever came here, which I don't suppose she did." There was a suspicion of a sniff at the end of the last remark.

" Well, madam," said the inspector, rising, " if you do see her now you're in London, I hope you'll let me know. I'm much obliged to you for your helpful information. Good morning, madam."

As he closed the drawing-room door behind him, he added to himself :

" So there's a woman in the case, is there ? We must add her to the list. *Cherchez la femme*, Mr. Dobson, *cherchez la femme*."

Unlocking the study, the inspector went in and assured himself that everything was as he had left it—as it was, that is, at the time of the tragedy—except that the french window had been closed and shuttered to keep out intruders.

Ringing for the butler, he inquired about the use of sealing-wax or any other explanation of the presence of candle-grease on the writing-table. Jackson was unable to give him any help; he had never known Sir John to use sealing-wax, nor had he ever seen a candle in the room. Alice, the head housemaid, confirmed this. She had never seen candle-grease in the room before. The inspector came to the conclusion that the intruder must have turned out the electric light and worked with a candle that he had with him, though why he should have switched on the light again before leaving was not apparent.

The detective next sent for P.C. Raffles, who had come on duty again that morning, and, locking the study door, explained to him the part he was to play in his proposed reconstruction of the crime. The police constable, with a rolled-up newspaper in his hand, concealed himself behind the curtain of the right french window, while the detective, opening the left window, went out on to the veranda. He then came back into the room and passed round the corner of the writing-table, on which the telephone was standing. As he did so, P.C. Raffles stepped quietly out from behind the curtain of the right window and struck him a violent blow on the back of the head with the rolled-up paper. Dobson collapsed on to the floor, his body covering, to a very fair extent, the outline chalked on the carpet by the detective on the previous day.

" That's quite hard enough, Raffles," said the detective, rising to his feet and rubbing the back of his head. " Try some lighter literature—I always thought the *Financial News* looked pretty heavy ! But, look here, you were a bit too soon. I saw you quite clearly before I turned the corner of the table."

The experiment was repeated, the constable this time delaying his blow until the detective's back was fully turned to him. The latter collapsed as before, but only his feet touched the chalk outline, the rest of his body being beyond it.

"That won't do," he said. "That's too late. Try again, and strike a happy medium—and don't strike it too hard."

Again, and yet again, the experiment was repeated, but every time either the "victim" could not fail to see his assailant emerging from behind the curtain, or else his body fell well beyond the chalk outline. The detective was frankly puzzled.

"Raffles," he said, "there's something odd here. Suppose you haven't got one of your brain waves about it?" The constable shook his head. "Well, it'll be something for the Superintendent to think about—that's more his job than mine."

Putting the matter out of his mind for the time being, Inspector Dobson sent for James, and questioned him more closely than he had previously done about his past history. The footman displayed no particular eagerness to divulge the details of his career, but gradually the detective drew from him an autobiography which was mainly notable for its variety of interests and the briefness of its connection with each. Evidently the young man was a rolling stone, who had tried one career after another, either tiring of each in turn or being tired of. Since the war he seemed to have made a definite attempt to settle down, but since the war that laudable ambition had become much more difficult of achievement and he had again passed from job to job and place to place until a few months ago, when he had been taken on in his present employment by Sir John Smethurst.

"But how did you get this job?" inquired the detective. "Mr. Jackson tells me you didn't come from a registry office, but that Sir John picked you up himself. Where did he find you and why did he give you the job?"

The footman replied that he had been acting as waiter in a restaurant car on the G.W.R., and that one day Sir John had come in to take luncheon in his car. He, James, had recognized him at once. He had served in the same battalion of the Royal Fusiliers as young Mr. John Smethurst, Sir John's only son, who had been killed at Paschendaele in '17, and had once acted as his batman for a short time while his regular batman was sick, and had seen a photograph of Sir John among his things. He had introduced himself to Sir John when the latter had finished his lunch, and as a result of the conversation Sir John had given him his present post.

Inspector Dobson did not feel altogether satisfied with this explanation, as it appeared to offer an insufficient reason for the appointment to a position of trust of a man so little suited for it. He therefore pressed James Riley and eventually elicited from him something which put the matter in quite a different light. This was that Riley had been employed as office boy in the engineering business in Oldham in which the young John Smethurst had gone bankrupt in 1900. Riley assured the detective that this had nothing to do with his being given the post, and that he had not even told Sir John of this earlier connection, but Inspector Dobson had his own views on that point, and made a mental note that it would be well worth while to pay a visit to Lancashire and investigate that early history.

Having disposed of this point, the detective turned his attention to the search for the weapon and the memorandum-book. He spent more than an hour searching first the garden of St. Margaret's Lodge and then the gardens of the adjoining houses—that part of them, that is to say, into which either of the missing articles might have been thrown by someone passing down the road. He had little hope of success, and he was not wrong. Deciding, at the end of an hour, that he was wasting his valuable time, he returned to the house and, calling P.C. Raffles into the study, instructed him to continue the search, and also to make inquiries as to any suspicious person having been seen in the neighbourhood on the night of the murder. He felt that he was asking the constable for needles in a haystack, but it was routine work that had to be done, and occasionally these blindfold searches struck oil.

He was leaving the study, when the door of the morning-room opposite opened and Mrs. Spurling appeared. When she saw the detective she beckoned to him excitedly, and drew him to the window of the morning-room, which looked on to the drive. On the gravel in front of the steps two women were talking.

" There ! " whispered the old lady excitedly ; " talking to my niece. The woman of the photograph ! "

" By Jove ! " cried the detective. " The Spanish Countess ! "

CHAPTER XII

SOME STEPS FORWARD

THINKING over this dramatic disclosure on his way to the City, Inspector Dobson came to the conclusion that, after all, there was really nothing very startling about it. Old gentlemen had been known to fall in love with beautiful ladies before now, and there was no reason why Sir John Smethurst, a widower for many years, should not also have fallen a victim to a belated affection of the heart. After all, the presence of her photograph in Sir John's cigarette-case in no way implied anything to the lady's discredit—she might even be unaware of its presence there. The assumption of impropriety had, in fact, been purely an assumption on the part of Mrs. Spurling—the kind of suggestion that appears to leap to the mind of the very pious or the very dull. In all probability, Sir John had fallen quite honourably in love, and if he were to do so, with whom could it more naturally be than the very beautiful woman who, as his daughter's greatest friend, was constantly in and out of his house.

The detective, a model of respectability, reproached himself for having allowed an evil thought to take such easy possession of his mind. " *Honi soit*," he felt, " *qui mal y pense*." Nevertheless, he determined tactfully to inquire, either from Miss Smethurst or from the lady herself, just how the matter stood.

Having, on the previous day, ascertained the name and address of Sir John's solicitors, Inspector Dobson went straight to their offices and sent in his card. He was received at once by the senior partner, Mr. Oswald Hogworthy, an elderly gentleman whose expression suggested a conflict between innate respect for the law and disdain for the particular branch of it which the inspector represented. Having introduced himself, the detective went straight to the point.

" I want to have a look at Sir John's will, Mr. Hogworthy," he said, " and perhaps make a note or two of its contents."

Mr. Hogworthy's face lengthened—if such a thing were possible.

" That is very unusual, Inspector," he replied ; " before the body is even interred. Most unusual. I trust that you will not press the point."

The inspector was respectful, regretful, but firm. He wanted briefly, to see the will now, and—he saw it. It was a commendably brief document. The testator left a year's salary or wages to everybody in his employ at the time of his death, a sum of twenty thousand pounds to his executors to be administered in accordance with instructions given to them separately, and, after a clause saying that he had given largely to charity during his life and proposed to leave it to the option of his heir to continue to do so, the residue absolutely to his daughter, Emily Charlotte Brontë Smethurst.

The detective thanked Mr. Hogworthy and, having obtained, grudgingly, the names of Sir John's executors, took his departure.

" That seems pretty straightforward," he said to himself. " I was afraid I might have to wade through twenty pages of lawyer's rigmarole. I'll tackle these executors while I'm on this line—they're pretty sure to be at the old man's office. And I can have another look for that memorandum-book while I'm there."

But if the inspector anticipated smooth running for his little plan, he was duly disillusioned. He found, in fact, that it was one thing to ride rough-shod over a London solicitor and quite another to try the same tactics with a Lancashire business man—still more with two. When he announced to Sir John's executors, Messrs. William Carple and James Spurgeon, that it was his desire to examine then and there the details of Sir John's confidential instructions to his said executors, touching the twenty thousand referred to in his will, he was told pleasantly but quite firmly to go and buy himself a new hat—or, by inference, to indulge in any pleasure or business beyond the purview of Messrs. Spurgeon and Carple that he might select.

The inspector tried reason, with absolutely negative results. The executors had received confidential instructions, and the executors had no difficulty in appreciating the meaning of the word " confidential."

The inspector next tried threats, mentioning the awful powers which would immediately be put into operation should reason be unavailing. The result was identical. Let the inspector subpœna them to produce their instructions at the inquest if he would ; the executors would take advice and keep within the laws of their country, but, short of such infringement, they were going to show their instructions to nobody. Knowing that he had no immediate power to enforce his will, the inspector departed, the wiser for a little knowledge of his fellow-countrymen, but for nothing else.

With the manager of the Exchange Branch of the City and Suburban Bank he was more successful, and with a minimum of delay he was closeted in a small office with a bulky volume—the details of Sir John's private account for the past five years—and a junior clerk, nominally to help, actually to watch him. The figures contained in this volume made him almost gasp, but it was a long time before he found anything to help him. Large sums, both on the credit and debit side, appeared against a great variety of names, some known, but the majority unknown to him. He made a list of the principal names and sums, hoping that he might in the course of his investigation run up against one of them in a more obviously significant connection. It was not until he was tabulating the cash payments—payments to " Self "—that he struck a definite line of suggestion. Sums of varying amounts from one hundred to two or three thousand pounds, had been drawn by the dead man at equally varying dates, but it suddenly struck the detective that one figure, that of £400, appeared at fairly regular intervals. He went back over the list and made a separate one, noting the dates on which each of these sums was drawn, with the result that there emerged the definite fact that for the last two years Sir John had been drawing the sum of £400 in cash at the beginning of each quarter, even though, as sometimes had happened, he had drawn large sums to " Self " within a few days.

Inspector Dobson spent some time considering the significance of this discovery. It might, of course, have no significance—be a mere routine habit ; on the other hand, it was suggestive and might mean much, even to the extent of blackmail. Regular cash payments on such a scale generally meant something interesting. Finally the detective asked if he might see the manager again, and the latter soon appeared. Dobson pointed out the figures to him and asked if he could throw any light on them, but the manager was unable to help him at all—even if he had been prepared to divulge any confidential information which he might have had. The detective had to content himself with a list of the numbers of the banknotes (£50) which had been paid out to these drafts at the last two quarters—July 1 and October 1, the latter, of course, within the last few weeks. With this information he felt it should not be impossible to trace the recipient of these payments—if regular payments to an individual were a correct assumption—for in a case of this gravity banks would be unlikely to withhold information of an even more confidential nature.

In spite of the progress he had made during the day, Inspector Dobson felt that it had all been progress of an inconclusive nature. The outcome of his experiments in the study with P.C. Raffles had been purely negative in character, though a negative result might be as suggestive as a positive. The rather dramatic disclosure of Sir John's romantic attachment to his daughter's friend—if, again, that was a safe assumption—might have some connection with the crime, but more probably it had not. The discovery that Miss Smethurst was sole heiress—with the exception of the comparatively small trust fund—of her father's great wealth was important, but was in no way startling, whilst the trust fund itself, the most interesting feature in the will, was still a closed book to him. The large and regular cash drafts were no less interesting, but, again, the work of attaching a meaning to them was still ahead of him. The detective was not really dissatisfied with his day as far as it had gone, but he felt that the superintendent might be.

His cavalier treatment by Sir John's executors had driven one object of his visit to the office out of his head. He now returned there, intending to avoid these fiery guardians of the dead man's trust and to confine himself to the humbler but more amenable Mr. Morrison. He found the chief clerk in a much more settled state of mind than on the previous day. So far from being nervous and excitable, Mr. Morrison appeared to have inhaled some of the air of Manchester, and was inclined to be slightly truculent. The detective had no difficulty, however, in dispelling that atmosphere, and within a short time was listening to a fairly coherent flow of gossip. This he did not check, as he thought it possible that some fact of importance might emerge from it ; and he was not mistaken. After dealing with the eccentricities of millionaires in general, and those of his late employer in particular, he passed on to consider the position and prospects of the staff, and, finally, came to rest upon one individual—the confidential secretary. An entirely unnecessary post, of course ; the work could be done as well, if not better, by the chief clerk, and, in fact, between themselves, was so done to a large extent.

"And you know, Inspector," Mr. Morrison proceeded, " I fancy that some such conclusion had already begun to dawn on Sir John. I do not wish to make trouble or to cast undue aspersions, but it had become noticeable latterly that things were not as they had been between my employer and Mr. Hastings."

"What's that?" ejaculated the detective, startled out of the attentive silence that he had set himself to maintain. " How can that be? I thought Mr. Hastings was engaged to Miss Smethurst and with her father's full approval."

"Oh, quite, Inspector, quite," replied Morrison. " That is undoubtedly the case, but that occurred some months ago, and it is of the last few weeks that I am speaking."

"But in what way, man? Did they have a quarrel, or what?"

"Oh no. There was no quarrel that I am aware of. But Sir John has been touchy in a way I have never known before, and it seemed to me that he wasn't on the friendly terms with Mr. Hastings that you'd expect with a son-in-law—and which there used to be. I may be wrong, of course; I just wondered whether Sir John thought he'd made a mistake."

Again a suggestion, and again inconclusive.

The inspector turned to the question of finance, and producing his two lists, the one of Sir John's holdings which he had taken from his office desk the previous day, the other the list of large receipts and payments which he had copied out in the bank an hour previously, he asked the chief clerk to elucidate them. But here he met with a surprise, for the chief clerk at once shut up like an oyster and referred him to the secretary, or, better still, to the executors. This was the last thing the detective wanted, so he gave it up as a bad job and turned his attention to the missing memorandum-book. Here Mr. Morrison was at once more communicative and more definite. He knew the book well; Sir John was constantly consulting it and making entries in it. Sir John always kept it in his pocket—there was no possibility of its being found lying about in the office. No, he never locked it up in his office desk; quite definitely, in the ten years during which he had worked for Sir John, Mr. Morrison had never seen him lock the book away in his office desk, or do anything with it but put it back in his pocket. The inspector could search the office if he liked, of course; Sir John's room would be the place to start, and no doubt the executors would not hinder him in the execution of his duty, but Mr. Morrison was quite positive that, wherever the book might be, it was not in 15, St. Swithin's Court.

As he walked away from the office, Inspector Dobson

asked himself why he had got it so firmly into his head that the book might be there—what had made him think that Sir John often locked it up in his office desk.

Suddenly he stopped and slapped his leg.

" I know why I thought that," he said. " Hastings told me so."

CHAPTER XIII

SOME STEPS NOWHERE

THE evening's conference between the inspector and his chief had resulted in two definite conclusions : the first was to advertise a reward for the recovery of the missing memorandum-book ; the second, to inquire very closely into the movements of Mr. Geoffrey Hastings between the hours of 11 p.m. and 12.30 a.m.—the limits fixed by the medical report—on the night of the murder.

With regard to the reward, it was thought best that this should be done through the dead man's relations, and as Miss Smethurst had already, at her first interview with Inspector Dobson, offered to do this, it was decided to ask her to place the matter in the hands of her solicitors with a view to their issuing notices to the Press and placarding the neighbourhood.

As to Geoffrey Hastings' movements, he had already given an account of them, and it was only necessary to check the accuracy of his account. It will be remembered that he had told the detective that, after saying good night to Sir John, he had taken a taxi off the rank in the next street, Blenheim Road, had driven to his Club, played bridge there till one, and then, after sitting on the Embankment for a time, in the hope of getting rid of a headache, had walked home to his flat, which he had reached at about three. It was, in its way, disappointing that the doubtful period in his account—the time when he had been wandering about London after leaving his Club, and before returning to his flat—was well outside the time limit. Still, it was quite possible that a hole could be picked in his alibi within those limits.

Inspector Dobson's first move was to the Blue Stocking. He realized that detectives were hardly *personæ gratæ* at West-End clubs, but he hoped, by the exercise of a little tact, to get five minutes' conversation with the hall porter. This functionary was at first inclined to refer such a delicate problem in etiquette to the secretary for instructions, but as the inspector's time was valuable an agreement on the point was reached through the medium of the Treasury. The detective, however, got very little value for his ten shillings. The head porter, as soon as he heard what the information was that was wanted, at once referred him to the night porter, who would come on duty at 9 p.m. The night porter lived at Brixton. No, no note was made of the time members entered or left the Club, but the night porter might possibly remember the movements of members as recently as two nights ago.

Inspector Dobson decided not to trek out to Brixton, but to leave the night porter until he came on duty again, and in the meantime to seek out the members with whom Hastings had said he had played bridge—Hastings had given him a list of their names—and to get confirmation, or otherwise, from them. He asked the hall porter for the addresses of these gentlemen, but here the hall porter was on firm ground—he had no doubts at all on this point—a letter would be forwarded, but an address could not be given. Not wishing to antagonize a possible ally, Inspector Dobson did not apply the pressure which was in his power, but instead, turning into the nearest public telephone box, looked up the names in the directory. Of the five names which Hastings had given him, two appeared in the book—one, that of Captain James Buby, having an address in King's Street, St. James'; the other, Mr. William Snecker, a private address in Mayfair and a business address in the City.

Judging that, of the two, the latter was the more likely to be found at this hour of the morning, Inspector Dobson set out for the business address of Mr. W. Snecker, and, up to a point, his luck seemed to have turned. Mr. Snecker, large, florid, and cigar-smoking, was at his office, was disengaged, was delighted to meet him, would be glad if he would take a cigar, and remembered quite well playing bridge with Mr. Hastings at the Blue Stocking a couple of nights ago. At this point, however, the inspector's luck once more deserted him. Mr. Snecker had cut into Hastings' table at about a quarter to twelve, quite roughly, might have been earlier, might have been later, but had only played one rubber, and, cutting out, had gone home. Left the Club? Oh, probably about quarter or half-past twelve. Had looked at an illustrated in the smoking-room for ten minutes or so before leaving, so could not say whether Hastings was still playing when he left.

The detective realized that all this amounted to was that Geoffrey Hastings *had* been playing bridge at his Club that night round about midnight. Nothing more definite could safely be assumed. His visit, however, was not entirely wasted, for he got from Mr. Snecker the address of one of the other card players—Mr. Algernon Hopladdy, Stock Exchange, E.C.

To the Stock Exchange, therefore, Inspector Dobson betook himself, and, after waiting half an hour while Mr. Hopladdy was searched for and found, he waited for another half-hour while Mr. Hopladdy (" Hullo, Algie, old son ") greeted friends and acquaintances passing in and out of the doors of that sacred edifice, holding the inspector's card in one hand and a long amber cigarette-holder in the other. However, at last Mr. Hopladdy's attention was

entirely—not a large matter—at his disposal. Oh yes;
Mr. Hopladdy remembered quite well playing bridge at
the Blue Stocking on Monday night—matter of fact, he
played there pretty well every night. Oh yes; Mr. Hopladdy remembered Mr. Geoffrey Hastings playing quite
well—matter of fact, old Geof played pretty well every
night, too. Was he sure he had been there on Monday?
Oh yes; matter of fact, they'd been to the Hilarity together
to see Peeps Hopton in that new show—jolly good show
it was, too. Jolly nice little thing, Peeps. Did the
inspector know her? Mr. Hopladdy would be delighted
to take him round behind at the Hilarity any night he
liked. What was that? Not possible they'd been to the
Hilarity on Monday night? No, by Jove, nor they had—
must have been Saturday. Had been to Sunningdale on
Monday, of course, and had played a couple of rounds
with Jack Spollish and not got back till rather late—dined
at the Club. Jolly good chap, old Jack, and no mean
golfer. Did the inspector? . . .

The inspector realized that if he wanted any definite
information he must himself take charge of the conversation. He did so, and after endless retrievings of Mr.
Algernon Hopladdy from conversational side-alleys, he
elicited the fairly definite information that Mr. Hopladdy
had sat down to bridge at the Club at about half-past nine
and had played steadily till "any old hour," probably
nearly two; that "old Geof" had cut in, probably about
the fifth or sixth rubber—might have been about eleven,
but Mr. Hopladdy really couldn't say—and had played
four or five rubbers and then faded away—Mr. Hopladdy
had no idea when.

Again, definite information that Hastings had played
bridge at his Club, and played it for a considerable time,
but nothing in the least definite as to the hours at which
he had begun and finished.

Once more the inspector sought a telephone-box, and,

ringing up Captain Buby's rooms in the hopes of obtaining some information as to his whereabouts, obtained it ; Captain Buby had left for Scotland the previous night— Camloch Lodge, Ardenoch, Aberdeenshire—no, not on the telephone, and—his informant believed—fifteen miles from the nearest call office.

This was becoming distinctly tiresome. The inspector decided that the time had come to stand no more nonsense. He therefore returned to the Blue Stocking and curtly demanded audience of the secretary. The secretary had gone and would not be back till after lunch.

Fuming with rage, but still in control of his judgment, the detective decided to cut clean off this line of inquiry, and give it time to become more accommodating. Having reached this conclusion, he jumped on a bus and within twenty minutes presented himself at the cab-shelter in Blenheim Road. Half a dozen taxi men were having their midday meal, and, having asked and obtained leave to join them, he sat down with a soup-plate of Irish stew and a steaming cup of coffee before him and told his new friends what he wanted. He could hardly have come to a better place. The Blenheim Road cab-shelter and rank were an institution as exclusive as the " Turf " ; a select dozen made it their headquarters and a stranger rarely, if ever, pulled up on its sacred precincts. Certainly not on Monday night, nor yet on Sunday nor Tuesday ; that " Old Bottlenose " the cook-caretaker-cum-telephone boy, could absolutely swear.

None of the half-dozen men present had picked up the fare that the detective described. As the meal proceeded, two more dropped in, one after the other ; neither had driven a gentleman to the Blue Stocking within recent memory. Of the four remaining, one had had engine trouble on Sunday and his car had been out of commission ever since ; one, " Boiler " Johnson, had had a touch of gout the previous day and had not turned up that morning ;

and the two others, Bill Wittons and Ernie Burstall, were still on the road.

Ascertaining the address of Mr. Boiler Johnson, and leaving a message for Messrs. Wittons and Burstall that they should communicate with him at the Yard, Inspector Dobson repaired to the little back street off the Finchley Road in which the Boiler was reputed to lodge. As soon as he knocked at the door indicated by a harassed-looking landlady, the inspector became aware that the Boiler was in working order.

" Come in, blank yer, and stop makin' that blankin' row on my dore."

The inspector presented himself and his thirst for knowledge.

" Ho ! a blankin' Nosey Parker, are yer ? " shouted the sufferer. " Well, ye ken blankin' well tike yer blankin' nose outside 'er my room." The next minute a yell of mingled pain and rage escaped from what was evidently the safety valve as the Boiler's bandaged foot came in contact with the corner of an ottoman.

Five minutes were spent in waiting for the steam to escape, and five more to bring the pressure down to a temperature which would allow of a little information being given off instead. Then it emerged that Mr. Johnson had been taken bad on Monday, not on Tuesday, " so 'ow the blankin' 'ell could 'e a bin out on the road on Monday night ? " Obviously he couldn't, so that ended that.

Returning to the Club, Inspector Dobson found that the secretary had just come in and would see him. Although the detective was kept waiting for a further ten minutes, the meeting, when it at last took place, was quite amicable. The secretary quite saw that under the circumstances the inspector must have the information he required, and took upon himself the responsibility of divulging the addresses of Mr. Dermot O'Morish and Colonel Rudde-Gill without reference to the committee. Mr. O'Morish's address was in fact, Dunawn House, Dronclum, Co. Cavan, I.F.S., and Colonel Rudde-Gill, 1, Duke's Mansions, Earl's Court, S.W. Mr. O'Morish was believed to be still in London, but the secretary did not know where he was staying. There should, however, be no difficulty in getting in touch with Colonel Rudde-Gill.

There was none. The manservant at the Colonel's flat, answering the detective's telephone call, replied that his master was still at lunch; the port and nuts had been put before him not twenty minutes ago. The inspector asked if he might come round and see the Colonel at once. The manservant replied that he would inquire. He was away from the instrument for some time and when he returned it was in a state of great agitation and with the news that his master had evidently had a fit of some kind as he was lying back in his chair, purple in the face, with his eyes " turned inside out," and the decanter grasped firmly in his right hand.

CHAPTER XIV

THE AFFAIRS OF A COUNTESS

IF Inspector Dobson's morning had been disappointing, he had no reason to complain of the afternoon. After the failure of his last attempt to check Hastings' story, he returned to Scotland Yard to ask the superintendent whether he ought to go North and seek out Captain Buby on the banks of the Don. The superintendent told him to ring up the Aberdeen police and get them to send a man out to Ardenoch to interview the captain—a simple solution which had not occurred to the inspector. Returning to his room, the latter found that a message had come through from the Blenheim Road cab-shelter to say that Wittons and Burstall had come in and that neither of them had driven a fare to the Blue Stocking on the night in question. This information, though actually negative in form, was of very positive value, for it meant that the first part of Hastings' alibi had broken down—all the men who had been on the Blenheim Road rank that night had been found, and none of them had driven him, as he had said, to his club. Still, the detective was not prepared yet to look upon Geoffrey's story as a fake ; it seemed absurd to suppose that anyone faking an alibi would begin it with a lie that could so easily be exposed and, in addition, the period of time covered was really too early to be vital. Quite possibly there would be a simple explanation of the failure—but Hastings would have to produce an explanation.

The inspector had not been in his office long when he received a message that a gentleman, a Mr. William Carple, had called and asked to see him on urgent private business. Wondering what this pugnacious trustee could want with him, the inspector gave orders for him to be admitted at once. Mr. Carple wasted no time in idle apologies. He was a plain man, and a busy one, and he went straight to the point. The two trustees had discussed the detective's threat to subpœna them to produce their confidential instructions regarding the twenty-thousand-pound trust at the inquest, and had come to the conclusion that it would be wiser to take the detective into their confidence and trust to his finding it possible to keep a rather delicate matter out of Court. The inspector heartily agreed with the wisdom of the decision, and without further ado the dead man's letter of instructions was put into his hands.

As in the case of the will, the document was short and simple. The trustees were asked to invest the capital according to their judgment and to administer the income to the best advantage of the Countess Barretta. On the death of the Countess, the capital was to revert to the dead man's estate.

The inspector with difficulty choked a whistle. Undoubtedly Sir John had been deeply attached to the beautiful widow. There was nothing to indicate any connection between the attachment and the crime, but the line was worth following up. In the meantime, he handed back the document to Mr. Carple with an assurance that if he found it possible he would keep the matter private.

When Mr. Carple had departed, the inspector went and told his superior of this new development and then betook himself to the block of flats in Queen Anne Street, where, he had ascertained, Madame Barretta lived. He did not venture to call upon the Countess herself, but he got into conversation with the porter who ruled over the block and from him gathered a good idea of the style of living of the inhabitants generally. There was, of course, considerable variety—some had Rolls-Royces and some merely used taxis—but there was no doubt at all that the general style of living was extremely comfortable. The inspector knew nothing about the means enjoyed by the widow of Count Barretta—but he was determined to find out.

His most promising source of information was either the Countess herself or her friend, Miss Smethurst, but the inspector was a cautious man and decided not to rush in precipitately where angels might fear to tread. He would think the matter over carefully and consult the superintendent, but in the meantime he could find out a good deal. Ascertaining from the porter the name and address of the firm of agents who controlled the flats, he walked the short distance that separated them and sent in his name to one of the partners. Mr. Pimmery, the junior—and juvenile—member of the firm, who alone happened to be in at the time, was evidently thrilled by a visit from a flesh-and-blood detective. He expressed willingness to help in every possible way and was clearly prepared to divulge any information, of however confidential a nature, which the inspector might require. His enthusiasm received a slight check when he learnt the name of the client whose secrets he was to divulge—evidently the Countess' charms had not been wasted upon him. But as the two questions which the inspector put to him appeared harmless enough, his momentary anxiety was quickly dispelled.

" Oh, yes, Inspector," he replied to the first. " On the nail always, I can assure you. I'll just make sure about the last half-year's." He rang a handbell and gave the necessary instructions to a respondent clerk. " You need feel no doubts about the Countess' financial soundness, I am convinced. We are always most particular about our tenants in the Queen Anne flats." The clerk returned. " Not received yet. Well, that's odd. But a mere over-sight, I have no doubt. We will, of course, communicate. . . ."

And to the second :

" Easily, my dear sir. Our accounts clerk will be able to tell you." Another ring. " Ah, here he is. Snush, what bank does the Countess Barretta bank with ? The Victoria and Vauxhall ? Thank you, that's all. There you are, Inspector. That really all you want ? Not at all ; very glad to be able to help you. Have a cigarette ? Well, good morning, and good luck."

Within ten minutes the inspector was again closeted with a bank manager. But this time his reception was anything but friendly. In fact, the manager of the Victoria Branch of the Victoria and Vauxhall absolutely declined to give him any information about his client's financial affairs. The inspector recognized that he was dealing with a man who was confident of his complete suzerainty in the kingdom over which he ruled. He abruptly bade him good morning, and, returning to Scotland Yard, obtained a search warrant, and within half an hour was back again. Without comment, he showed the warrant to the manager, and the latter, after turning first red and then white, ordered the necessary books to be brought.

As it was something more than an inspection of books

that he wanted, the detective thought it wise now to apply a little soft soap.

"I quite understand your attitude in the matter, Mr. Crabbitt," he said, giving the manager a friendly nod. "It is, of course, quite right that you should defend your clients' interests. I saw that you were not a man to surrender the fort lightly, so I thought the only fair thing to you was to bring up a piece of artillery that you could not possibly resist. You have done your duty, and I equally have done mine. I hope you bear me no ill will?"

Mr. Crabbitt was mollified.

"No, Inspector. I see that you had to do it," he said. "If I can help you, let me know."

"That's all right, then," replied the inspector. "I shan't be a minute looking through this. Ah, here we are. Credit side. £400 a quarter is the principal item, I see. Now, could you tell me—oh, yes, I see; paid in in cash. By the lady herself? Yes, I thought so. Now, could you tell me" (he produced from his pocket the list of the numbers of the bank notes drawn by Sir John Smethurst on the last two occasions) "whether any of these notes were included in the cash payments on the last two occasions? You would keep a list of the numbers, wouldn't you?"

Mr. Crabbitt took the list and left the room. Within five minutes he was back again.

"That, Inspector," he said, "is an exact list of the notes paid in by the Countess Barretta on July 1st and October 1st this year."

Inspector Dobson replaced the list in his pocket with a grim smile.

"Ye'es," he said; "I thought it might be. Frailty, thy name is—Rosamund," he added under his breath. "A very comfortable little arrangement."

For a few minutes he sat thinking. It would evidently be a delicate matter, now, to approach either the Countess herself or Miss Smethurst on the subject. The Countess was likely to be reticent, and it was a hundred to one against Miss Smethurst having even an inkling of what had been going on between her father and her friend. The inspector, too, was human enough to be loath to add to the girl's misery by revealing to her, unless it was absolutely necessary, this sordid bit of treachery. It was still improbable that this newly revealed relationship had anything to do with Sir John's death, but the inspector thought it worth while to ask the bank manager one or two more questions.

" I don't want to go nosing into your client's account unless I can help it, Mr. Crabbitt," he said. " Now, would you just tell me this in confidence ? Have you had any difficulty with the Countess over her account—has she kept within reasonable limits, for instance ? "

The manager remained silent for a time. He was evidently thinking pretty deeply. At last he turned to the detective.

" Now, look here, Inspector," he said, " you give me your word that this information is absolutely necessary to you in your investigation of the murder of Sir John Smethurst ? "

" That's a fair question," replied the detective, " and I'll give you a fair answer. Either this information proves to be essential, or, if it does not, I give you my word that it goes no further."

" All right," said Mr. Crabbitt. " I'll tell you the facts. Up to five or six months ago, the Countess' account was quite in order. Then her debit side began to outweigh her credit. It was not that her ordinary bills—dressmakers' and so on—seemed to increase, but she drew several large cheques to " Self." After a couple of months I had to write to her about the state of her account, but I got no answer. Then, as the state of affairs continued, I took advantage of one of her visits to the bank to ask her to come and speak to me. I explained to her that the bank was anxious to show her all possible consideration, but that her overdraft had reached a size which made it necessary for us to ask for a definite arrangement to be made in the matter. She wasn't an easy lady to talk to—in fact, she seemed to think that I was being impertinent, but it had some effect, because she paid in enough cash to wipe off a considerable portion—half, I think—of the overdraft. I don't, of course, know where the cash came from. . . ."

" Got the numbers of the notes ? " interjected the detective.

" I can get them for you. Well, that was all right for the time being, but it didn't last. Last month she drew two small cheques—fifty pounds, I think—and then a large one, two or three hundred pounds, which we had to refuse. The directors will be considering the matter at their next meeting."

Inspector Dobson thanked Mr. Crabbitt for his help and promised to do his best not to reveal what he had learnt. As he left the building he muttered to himself :

" Looks as if you wanted money pretty bad, my lady. Now, I wonder whether you knew about that will."

CHAPTER XV

" YOU SHALL NOT HAVE HER ! "

RETURNING once more to Scotland Yard, Inspector Dobson got out the Summary which the superintendent and he had prepared on the first night. Reading through the fifth paragraph—" Points to follow up "—he was depressed to find what little progress he had made, in spite of all his hard work. He had found neither the weapon nor the memorandum-book. He could give no definite explanation of the presence of candle-grease on the writing-table, nor could he answer any of the conundrums about cigarettes and cigars. He did not know who had lain in the geranium-bed and opened the scullery window—but since his experiments with P.C. Raffles in the study, both he and the superintendent had inclined to the idea that the answer to this question was the answer to the whole problem, so that it was perhaps unreasonable to expect it to be found in a hurry. Finally, he had not yet investigated Sir John's financial undertakings, apart from the matter of the cash payments to the Countess Barretta.

The only point which he definitely knew all about was the third. He knew all about the will, and here again it only led him to the Countess—a line which, in spite of its rather dramatic nature, he felt instinctively was a blind alley. However, he added her name, and the facts that he had discovered about her, to the list of " Prominent Persons."

Having done so, he cast his eye over the rest of the list, and at once began to cheer up. In the matter of Geoffrey Hastings he had made undoubted progress—indefinite, it was true, but suggestive. Hastings' story, although it could not be said to have absolutely broken down under his examination, had quite certainly not been confirmed. He had been singularly unfortunate in his witnesses to the Blue Stocking section of the story, and there was still a good deal that might be cleared up under this head, but the taxicab section had definitely broken down—though the inspector was very sceptical about this period being vital. But the point about Hastings that really interested him was the information that Morrison, the chief clerk, had given him about the coolness, if not actual hostility, that had arisen between Sir John and his secretary. Of course, the story might be quite untrue, attributable to imagination or to the deliberate invention of a jealous subordinate—the detective did not altogether like what he had seen of Mr. Morrison—but if it were true—and surely if it were it should not be impossible to obtain confirmation—here was a very definite suggestion of a motive ; a man (past history as yet unknown, the inspector noted with a sigh) is engaged to the sole heiress of a millionaire ; then, owing to the hostility of the father, there is a sudden prospect that the marriage may not take place ; an unscrupulous man might not shrink from murder to remove this danger.

The inspector determined to lose no time in investigating the past history of Mr. Geoffrey Hastings, and to seek confirmation of the story of his quarrel with his employer—particularly as to the possibility of its having reached a pitch endangering his engagement to Miss Smethurst.

As if in answer to his thoughts, the inspector at this point received a message that a Mr. Herbert Wollop had called to see him, as he had what he thought might be a useful bit of information to give him about Sir John Smethurst. Mr. Wollop proved to be a small person, of a cheerful countenance and an odour redolent of the soil.

" Good evening, guv'nor," he said, as the detective waved him to a chair. " I've not been much in the way of you gentlemen—not sorry for it, and no hoffence meant," he added with a chuckle. " I may be takin' of a liberty, but I thought I maybe hought to run along with my little bit o' news. It's like this 'ere. I'm a gardener in Regent's Park—not a bad job, heither, fair pay and reg'lar work, but that's as may be. Has I was sayin', I works in Regent's Park and this hafternoon I sees a notice outside one o' the gates about a pocket-book wot's missin'. I got talking to one o' my mates about it an' 'e says as 'ow 'e believed it 'ad to do with a murder up Blenheim Road way—gen'lman o' the name o' Smeller, or somethin' like it—'e'd 'eard there'd bin a cop round the gardings up there lookin' for a pocket-book. Now, I'm not much of a one for the news-papers meself—'ceptin' for the football an' the 'orce-racin' —and I 'adn't seen nothin' about this 'ere murder. But my mate, 'e shows me a paper wot as' a picture o' this 'ere

Smeller in it, an' I sees at once 'as it's a gentleman as I've hoften seen in the Park."

Mr. Wollop paused for breath and automatically passed his sleeve over his mouth. The detective relaxed his look of intense interest.

" Do with a glass ? " he asked.

Mr. Wollop's eyes widened as the inspector rose from his chair and, going to a cupboard in the corner of his room, took out a bottle of Bass and a tumbler.

" Strike me ! " ejaculated the gardener of Regent's Park as the foaming glass was put into his hand. " This ain't such a bad shop to come to hafter all—if yer comes to the right dore," he added significantly.

" Well, has I was sayin'," he went on, putting the half-empty glass on the table in front of him, " I knows this 'ere Smeller well by sight."

" Smethurst," interjected the pained detective ; " Sir John Smethurst."

" Smithers, is it ? " replied Mr. Wollop. " Well, this 'ere Smithers, I know 'im well by sight, an' I remembers somethin' about 'im that might be in your line. O' course, I don't know as what I tells you 'as got hanythin' to do with the pocket-book as there's a reward for." Mr. Wollop's pause was clearly interrogatory, but as the inspector remained silent, he continued : " Well, this is what it is. One day about a fortnight hor three weeks ago, I was in my tool'ouse wot's be'ind some shrubs back o' the Botnical Gardins, when I 'ears voices comin' from the seat the hother side o' the shrubs. This 'ere seat's some way hoff the path and folks sittin' on it would think they was private-like—they wouldn't know about my little tool-'ouse. Well, I didn't take much notice of what they was sayin' till presently it come over me that they was gettin' a bit riled like—at least, one of 'em was. An' jus' as I come to notice that, I 'eard one of 'em sing hout : ' You shan't 'ave 'er ; by God, you shan't.' "

The inspector drew in his breath sharply and shifted farther forward in his chair. Mr. Wollop, as if conscious of the dramatic value of a pause, deliberately took a drink from his glass and set it down empty. But the inspector was blind now to human wants.

"Well, man, what next?" he urged. "Go on; go on."

Mr. Wollop, looking slightly aggrieved, continued :

"Well, o' course, that made me prick up me hears. But I didn't get no more. Another chap seemed to be talkin', but I couldn't catch what 'e said. 'E seemed to be trying to cool the other chap down, reasonin' with 'im like. Then there wasn't any more talkin' an' I puts me 'ead round a bush to see wot's 'appenin', and there was one chap walkin' away over the grass towards the Zoo and on the seat there was this chap Smellers, or Smithers, or whatever you calls 'im. 'E was lookin' all white an' shaky and I thought 'e was going to cry, but presently up 'e gets and goes hoff towards Hanover Gate, mutterin' to 'imself."

Mr. Wollop stopped. His tale was told. But for Inspector Dobson it still lacked its point.

"But the other chap," he cried ; "the chap that walked away towards the Zoo! Who was he? What was he like?"

"Oh, I don't know 'oo 'e was. Never set eyes on 'im before," returned Mr. Wollop.

"But what was he like, man?"

"Oh, 'e was like pretty well most o' the young chaps wot walks across the Park of an evenin' on their way back from work." Mr. Wollop's tones suggested that he had told a good story and it was ridiculous to expect him to add frills to it.

"Oh, he was young, was he? What sort of age would you say?"

"Ah, there, I can't tell you. Yer see, 'e was fifty or sixty yards away an' 'ad 'is back to me. I didn't see 'is fice."

" Well, what sort of build was he, then ?   Tall, short, fat, thin, well-set up ? "

" Well, 'e was sort of middlin' 'eight.   I shouldn't say 'e was very fat, nor yet very thin.   'E 'eld himself pretty well. 'E was wearin' a dark sort of suit," added Mr. Wollop, as if this ought to clench the description, " an' one o' them trilby hats—or was it a bowler ?   Well, it was one or t'other ;   I couldn't say which."

The inspector collapsed in his chair, his face a picture of baffled anticipation.   What a hopeless description of a man in London !   It might cover any one of half a million. And yet, was it so hopeless ?   It certainly might be said to describe Geoffrey Hastings.   He tried the effect of a second bottle of beer upon Mr. Wollop, but beyond the fact that the unknown man looked as if he might have been a " gent," Mr. Wollop was unable to give him anything more definite.

" Well, anyhow, Wollop," said the inspector at last, " you've given me a useful piece of information.   I don't suppose it'll qualify you for the pocket-book reward, but if there's any reward offered for the murderer of Sir John Smethurst and your news turns out to mean what I think it does, I'll see you get your share of it."

Mr. Wollop thanked him and, with a happy smile on his face and the suspicion of a hiccup in his voice, departed.

The inspector at once took his news to the superintendent. The latter listened to Mr. Wollop's story in silence and then asked for the rest of the day's results.   When the detective had finished, the superintendent sat for ten minutes looking at the desk in front of him.

" Well, Dobson," he said at length, " you've done a useful day's work.   I'm not sure this Countess business may not mean more than you think, but, in any case, the important thing at the moment is to get on to this Hastings line.   Hunt up his back history and get some corroboration about the quarrel story."   He paused, and then went on. " Now, look here ;   tell you what I'd do.   My experience

is that a frontal attack gets through nine times out of ten
—sometimes it scares a chap off, but more often it frightens
him into giving himself away. Go straight for him, tell
him what you've heard about this quarrel, and ask him
point-blank for an answer—don't give him time to think.
Then tell him about his alibi breaking down, then get him
to explain that. Stick to him, worry him, and watch him—
you can often get more from a look or a movement than
from an answer—unconscious, you know. And put one of
your chaps on to keep an eye on him—mustn't lose sight
now. You've had a long day, but strike while the iron's
hot. Off you go."

The inspector needed no incitement. He felt that he
had really got on to a hot scent now, and he was keen to
follow it up. It was nearly eight o'clock, though, and he
had eaten nothing but a sandwich since breakfast. He
knew that he had got a long case in front of him and that
he would want all his strength and staying power before
it was over, so he decided to get himself a square meal
before hunting up his quarry. Like a wise man, too, he
took his time over it, so that it was nearer nine than eight
when he was ready to start. He had decided not to use
the telephone in his search for Hastings, as he wanted to
take him by surprise, and in any case he felt fairly confident
that he would find him at St. Margaret's Lodge.

Geoffrey Hastings had had a trying day with the two
trustees, who, being business men, would take nothing for
granted, and, being really very ignorant of finance on the
scale with which they were now dealing, took a long time
to grasp what the secretary was trying to explain to them.
Geoffrey had been looking forward all day to a quiet evening
alone with Emily, so that it can be imagined that he was
not too well pleased when, at a quarter-past nine, their
tête-à-tête dinner barely finished, Jackson announced the
unexpected arrival of Inspector Dobson.

" Oh, hell ! " said Geoffrey. " Sorry, Em. Show him

94

into the drawing-room, Jackson, and tell him I'll be along presently. I must have my coffee."

"I beg your pardon, sir, but the inspector said the matter was urgent."

"Oh, all right," groaned the unfortunate Geoffrey. "I'll come. I'm so sorry, darling. I'll shove him off as quickly as ever I can."

Inspector Dobson remained standing after Geoffrey had greeted him, which compelled the latter to do the same. Without beating about the bush, he told Geoffrey that it had come to his ears that there had been a quarrel between him and his employer and that Sir John had threatened to break off the engagement. As he spoke he saw the face which he was watching suddenly stiffen and set like a rock, but whether it was from fear or anger he could not tell. There might have been fear in that look; when Hastings spoke, however, there was no doubt about the anger.

"Look here, Inspector," he cried; "I don't know where you got this cock-and-bull story from, but it seems to me that you've got your knife into me, and I want to know what it's all about. Are you accusing me of killing Sir John?"

"Would you mind answering my question, sir, please?" replied the detective quietly. "Was there a quarrel between you and Sir John, and did he threaten to break off your engagement?"

For answer Geoffrey walked to the bell and pressed it.

"Ask Miss Smethurst if she will be so good as to join me here," he said to the butler, who answered the bell.

One glance showed Emily that there was something seriously amiss, and she looked anxiously at her lover's face.

"The inspector wants to know, Emily, whether your father had a quarrel with me and wanted to break off our engagement."

Emily's eyes flashed as she turned to the inspector.

" What nonsense ! " she said. " My father loved Geoffrey nearly as much as he did me."

But the inspector was not finished.

" We'll leave that point at the moment, then, sir. Now, will you please tell me this ? Were you aware that the lady to whom you were engaged was the sole heiress to all her father's wealth ? "

For a moment Emily was afraid that her lover was going to knock the detective down. His eyes blazed and he half lifted his clenched fist. But he regained control of himself, and his voice was quiet—deadly quiet—when he answered.

" You are suggesting that I am marrying Miss Smethurst for her money. Perhaps you will change your mind when I tell you that I knew—have known for months—that her father was on the verge of bankruptcy ! "

CHAPTER XVI

A NEW DEVELOPMENT

It would be difficult to say which of the two—Emily Smethurst or Inspector Dobson—was the more taken aback by the astounding statement that Geoffrey Hastings had just made. Emily was the first to recover her speech.

" Geoffrey ! " she cried. " What can you mean ? Daddy nearly bankrupt ? "

" I'm afraid so, darling. It has been hanging over him for some time. The Russian business started it—he had big holdings in Russia before the war and, of course, they were a dead loss. Then came the slump in the mark. He had tremendous reserves, of course, or he'd have gone under at once, but he had to cut his losses, and that left him without a margin. He's been fighting like a tiger to get back, but luck's been against him and he's been losing ground. I've seen it coming for weeks, but I don't believe he did—he was a typical Britisher—never knew when he was beaten. It would have broken him if he had gone down—it's been almost merciful, this."

Geoffrey stopped. The excitement that had fired him to begin seemed to die out as his story ended. He looked tired and old, but, at the same time, relieved. He seemed like a man who had been carrying a great weight and, now that it had fallen from him, was half distressed at his failure to carry it and half thankful to be free of the burden.

Emily had sunk into a chair and was frankly crying. When Geoffrey stopped she looked up.

"Oh, poor daddy," she said. "Why didn't he tell me? It must have been dreadful for him to have that hanging over him, and of course he'd have been worrying most about me and of course it wouldn't have mattered to me a bit. Oh," she cried, "that's what has been the matter with him! I thought he'd been worrying about something. Don't you remember I talked to you about it three or four weeks ago, and you said you'd noticed something yourself?"

Inspector Dobson, who had remained silent out of respect for the feelings of the girl on whom this further blow had fallen, now decided that it was time for him to take a hand.

"Excuse me, miss," he said, "you never told me anything about that. Nor did you, sir "—turning to Geoffrey —" though I particularly asked you both if you'd noticed anything unusual about Sir John."

"You asked me if he ever gave me reason to suppose he had enemies who might mean mischief to him," answered Emily. "It never occurred to me that you meant anything of this kind—just worried. It never entered my head."

"That may be so, miss; but what about you, sir?

You never said a word to me about this bankruptcy, or even about his being in difficulties."

"That's true enough, Inspector," replied Geoffrey, "and I suppose I wasn't quite frank with you, but I didn't see what it could possibly have to do with the murder, and I couldn't blurt the whole thing out before seeing the executors. Don't you see that if it had got about, the whole fat would have been in the fire and there would have been an almighty panic? A man like Sir John has got a great deal more than his own troubles to bear—thousands of people depend on him. If it had suddenly got about that he was bankrupt, all the concerns he was financing would have slumped at once, and, literally, thousands of people would have been ruined. We—the executors, that is—have been working night and day to see how we can let things down gradually so that other people won't suffer too much. I hope to God, Inspector, you won't let this get about unless it's absolutely necessary."

The inspector remained silent for a while.

"I see your point, sir," he said at last; "but it was a pity you didn't tell me at once and trust me to keep it quiet if I could. As it is, you've put yourself in the wrong and you may have hindered me—I hope, for your sake, you haven't. Now, look here, sir," he continued after another pause; "this news has taken the wind out of my sails in one direction, I'm free to admit, but there's more yet that's got to be cleared up, and I should advise you to help me to do it. I'll leave the question of this quarrel for the moment and come to the alibi. I've checked your story of your movements on Monday night, and I'll tell you frankly that I'm not satisfied. In the first place, every driver who was on the Blenheim Road rank that night denies having driven anyone to the Blue Stocking; and in the second, though there's evidence that you were at your club for some time, probably round about midnight, not one of your friends whose names you gave me can say what time you got there or when you left."

"But, Inspector," cried Geoffrey, "how can that be so? There were five or six fellows who were there, one or other of them, all the time with me. They must know pretty well when I was there."

"Not that I've been able to find out, sir. It's true that I haven't been able to get hold of two of them yet—Captain Buby is in Scotland, and Colonel Rudde-Gill was taken ill just when I was going to see him—and I haven't seen the night porter yet, but the others—Mr. Snecker and Mr. Hopladdy——"

"Oh, Algy," interposed Geoffrey impatiently; "he's a damn fool. But Jimmy Buby—he was in the Club when I got there—saw me arrive, I believe."

"Well, sir, if that's so, it's all to the good. We shall probably hear from him any time now—the Aberdeen police are in touch with him." Geoffrey winced. "I'm sorry, sir, it had to be done—he was the last one we could hope to get anything definite out of. As I say, we may hear from him any time now. In the meantime, if there's anything more you can tell me that will help to prove your story, so much the better."

Geoffrey remained silent for a while, looking into the fire with a frown on his face. Emily watched him anxiously. At last, turning to the inspector, he said:

"Look here, Inspector, I'd like to know just where I am. Am I 'under suspicion,' or whatever it's called? Have you got a warrant for me in your pocket?"

"Oh, no, sir," replied the detective in a shocked voice. "If that was so I should have warned you—'What you say may be used in evidence against you'—you know! No, sir; nobody's under suspicion—or, rather, everybody is. You told me what your movements were on the night of the murder; it was my duty to check your statement; I did and it didn't—or doesn't so far, at any rate—hold water. And there were one or two other things that wanted explaining—some of them you've explained this evening. That's the position. I've got to clear up the doubt about your story, and it will be all to your advantage to help me."

" I see," said Geoffrey. " All right. Now then, what's the trouble about my story ? You said you'd proved I hadn't taken a taxi from Blenheim Road ? Well, I don't know how you prove it, because I did. By Jove ! I know what's wrong. You said I hadn't taken a taxi off the rank, didn't you ? Well, I didn't. I remember now ; the chap had pulled into the curb at this end of the road—doing something to his light, I think. I took him because he was a good deal nearer than the rank. Wouldn't that solve the difficulty ? "

" It would, sir—if we can find him. I suppose you didn't notice the number, or anything of the kind ? "

" I didn't," replied Geoffrey. " Who ever does ? But I believe it was a new car—one of those ones with a lot of glass—probably one of the new ' H. and K.'s—there are a fair number of them on the streets now. We might be able to trace them, mightn't we ? "

" Easily, sir. I hope you're right—it will save a lot of trouble about that point. But what about the other ? Of course, Captain Buby may be able to tell us, but even then it would be better to have corroboration. There's this Mr. O'Morish, too, but he seems to have disappeared into the blue. You don't happen to know where he's living in London, do you ? "

" I don't, Inspector. I don't know him—first time I'd met him—that night. But they'd know at the club."

" They don't, sir. They only know his Irish address, which, of course, isn't much good. Oh, by Jove, there's that night porter, I haven't seen him yet—he might be able to help. I'll run along there now ; care to come with me ? "

" Of course I'll come," replied Geoffrey, jumping up.

" I want to get this off my chest." Then turning to Emily he continued. " Em, darling, you ought to get to bed early—you're tired out. But if you like I could ring you up and tell you if the inspector loves me any better." He laughed cheerfully, but Emily did not respond. She was looking straight before her, and was evidently so deeply lost in thought that she had not heard him speak to her. Then, as if conscious of the silence, she came to herself with a start, and jumped up from her chair.

" I'm coming, too," she said.

Geoffrey remonstrated with her, and the inspector looked none too well pleased, but she cut short all argument.

" Do you think I could sleep with this hanging over you ? " she said.

Her point of view was so intelligible that Geoffrey made no further attempt to stop her. A message was sent to the garage, and within five minutes a luxurious Daimler was at the door. In ten more they were outside the Blue Stocking. At the detective's request, Geoffrey stayed in the car with Emily.

" I'll come and tell you directly I've got what I want from him. Wouldn't do for you to be there," said the inspector.

Fortunately it was a quiet time in the Club, for the members who had dined there had either gone home or were playing bridge or talking in the smoking-room, whilst the theatres were not yet out. The inspector, therefore, had no difficulty in getting a quiet word with the night porter. The latter had evidently been warned by the head porter that the detective wanted to see him, and he had his facts ready.

" There's no difficulty about the time Mr. Hastings left," he said. " It's a rule here that anyone not sleeping in the Club is fined if he keeps it open after midnight—so much for every hour—and it's my job to note the time members go out after twelve. Here it is in the book, you see—' Mr. Hastings 1.5 a.m.' Other names, too, you see—some as late as two—Mr. Hopladdy the last, as usual. But I've got no record of when they came in, and I don't remember Mr. Hastings coming in that night, nor yet do the hall boys, because I've asked them. If it was anywhere between 11 and 12 it's not surprising, because there's a stream of them coming in and out then—from the theatres, you know, and so on. No, I'm sorry—I can't help you about that— I've thought about it ever since Mr. Spuke told me what you wanted to know, and I can't say more than that."

And with that the inspector had to be content. It was good evidence, clear and unquestionable, as far as it went, but it still left the crucial period unaccounted for. Slowly he returned to the waiting Daimler and its anxious occupants. He got inside and shut the door so that the chauffeur could not hear what he said.

" It's all right as far as it goes, sir," he said. " The night porter's got your name in the book as leaving at five minutes past one. But he doesn't know when you came in, nor yet do any of the other servants. And that's the time that worries me—that's the crucial time."

" What's the crucial time ? " asked Geoffrey.

The detective paused before replying. Then, looking closely at Geoffrey's face, he said deliberately :

" Between half-past eleven and twelve, sir ; possibly half an hour each side of that."

Geoffrey felt Emily shudder beside him, but she said nothing. He himself remained silent, and the inspector, after a pause, went on :

" Well, sir, we must hope for something from Captain Buby to-morrow, and we must try and find that taxi of yours. Now, I'll wish you good night." He spoke cheerfully, but there was a dry note in his voice. He had half risen from the little seat facing the other two when Emily put out her hand and stopped him.

"Wait a minute, please," she said, and her voice sounded strained and nervous. The inspector sat down again, and she continued : "I think I must tell you something. I haven't said anything about it till now, because it seemed so impossible, and I knew Geoffrey would be so upset. But I must tell you now—I had no idea that you could— that any one could suspect Geoffrey. There was someone else in the house on Monday night—only for a minute, but it was about the time you said—the crucial time, you called it—about half-past eleven."

The two men stared at her in astonishment. The detective was the first to speak.

"Who was it, miss ? " he said eagerly.

"Mr. McCorquodale," she replied.

CHAPTER XVII

BEGINNING AFRESH

OUTSIDE a West-End club at eleven o'clock at night is hardly a place for confidences, so the Daimler was driven into the Mall and pulled to the side in a quiet spot, and there, the three of them seated in the closed car while the chauffeur walked patiently up and down out of ear-shot, Emily told her story. It was simple enough. On Monday night she had been, as she had already told the inspector, to a play with a party of friends, intending to go on to a dance at Prince's afterwards. Coming out of the theatre, however, she had felt unwell and cried off the dance, telling her friends to go on without her. Mr. McCorquodale, however, had insisted on accompanying her home to see that she was all right, and as she had not felt up to arguing, she allowed him to do so, although she had not at all wanted his company. Arrived at St. Margaret's Lodge, she had let herself in with her latch-key. Mr. McCorquodale had followed her into the hall, saying something about handing her over to her maid, but she had told him that her maid would not be up, and he had then said good night. She had gone straight upstairs to bed, and he had left the house after saying good night to her.

Emily Smethurst paused for a moment, and then went on hurriedly, as if to anticipate the inevitable question :

" I haven't said anything about it before because he was only in the house for a second, and, in any case, it's impossible that he could have killed my father—and Geoffrey —Mr. Hastings—hated him, and daddy didn't like him, and it seemed awful that I should have had him in the house, practically against daddy's wishes, on the very night he was killed. I knew you would be furious, Geof, at his taking me back, and it seemed so trivial and I didn't think I need rake it up, and . . ." the halting sentence trailed away into silence. She looked miserably at Geoffrey, and saw on his face a look that frightened her ; she looked at the detective and saw a different look, but one that frightened her hardly less—a scowl of annoyance mingled with a gleam of eagerness—eagerness to get on this new trail and hunt down the wretched man who had made it.

The detective was the first to speak. His face had quickly recovered its normal appearance, and his voice was calm.

" You said that this gentleman, Mr. McCorquodale, left the house when you went upstairs, miss. Are you quite sure he did leave the house ?   Did you see him go ? "

" Oh, yes, of course. At least . . . Oh, yes, I must have."

" Look here, miss," said the detective.   " I want you to think carefully about this, and not say anything you aren't absolutely certain of. Now, about this gentleman, when he said good-bye to you, did he turn straight round and go out of the door while you were still looking at him ? "

Emily thought for a moment. Then : " No," she said.
" I turned round and went up the stairs, and I think he
watched me begin to go up—perhaps to see whether I
could manage them all right—though I wasn't really as
bad as all that." She paused again, and the detective could
see that she was concentrating her whole mind on the
effort of recollection. " When I was half-way up," she
continued, " I heard the front door slam, and I think—
—yes, I am sure I did—I looked round and he was
gone."

" Could he have slammed the door and then hidden
behind something—a curtain or a chair ? "

" I don't think so—there's nothing much in the hall
that he could hide behind. And I think I must have
looked round at once."

The detective sat for a minute, frowning at the window
in front of him. Suddenly a thought seemed to strike him.

" How does your front door fasten, miss ? Can it be
opened from the outside if it isn't latched ? "

" It's always kept latched—a Yale lock—my father and I
had keys. Otherwise you would have to ring."

" Yes, but Yale locks can be latched back so that they
don't catch. Then the door is only held by the ordinary
handle. Question is whether even so your door could be
opened from the outside or whether it has no handle on
the outside."

" It has a handle on the outside—in the middle of the
door. But the Yale lock is always kept latched so that it
has to be unlocked before you can get in from the outside."

" By Jove, Inspector," broke in Geoffrey. " I believe
I see what you are getting at. You think McCorquodale
put back the catch of the Yale lock while Miss Smethurst
was going upstairs with her back to him, then went out,
slamming the door behind him—and only the ordinary door
handle catching—and then after a bit simply turned the
outer handle and walked in again."

" That's about it, sir," replied Inspector Dobson. " I take it that that would be possible, miss ? "

" I suppose it would. But don't you see what you're implying ? Why should Mr. McCorquodale want to kill my father ? "

" Ah, miss ; that's another matter. That'll be for me to find out. I take it you don't know of anything, miss. What about you, sir ? " He turned suddenly to Geoffrey.

The latter frowned.

" That's asking rather a lot, Inspector," he said. " If you ask me why I hate the sight of the chap—and Sir John didn't like him much better—I could tell you quick enough, but that's rather a different thing from fixing a murder on him. Of course, as you know, the swine was running after Miss Smethurst—not that one would blame him for that, but he went on after we were engaged. And I suppose he knew well enough that she was her father's heiress—and you tried to fasten that on to me as a motive for killing my best friend "—Geoffrey's voice was bitter— " so I suppose it applies equally to him—and he certainly didn't know about the bankruptcy. Mind you, Inspector," he added, " I'm not suggesting that as a motive ; I'm merely shifting the cap from my head to his."

" I understand that, sir," said the detective. " Just one thing more, miss. You said it was about half-past eleven that you said good night to this gentleman. Can you fix the time exactly ? "

" I'm afraid I can't. We came out of the theatre soon after eleven. It took a little time to get a taxi, and I suppose the drive is about a quarter of an hour. I have a vague recollection of seeing a clock at half-past eleven when I got home, but I can't be certain."

Inspector Dobson grunted. " Better if you could be quite sure. Think it over, miss, and see if you can't fix it."

" Well," he continued. " I must look into this. I'm sorry to have kept you so long, miss, though the extra time hasn't been altogether my fault." There was a twinkle in his eye as he spoke. "I suppose I ought to say something about your not telling me this story before, but I know you've had a bad time, and I'm not going to. I don't know, of course, what they'll say about it at the Yard. Well, good night, miss; good night, sir—I'll let you know if I hear from Captain Buby."

The two watched the detective's broad back disappear into the gloom beyond the nearest lamp-post. Then Emily turned to Geoffrey and touched his arm.

" Darling," she said, " I'm so terribly sorry. What will you think of me ? "

Geoffrey turned to her eyes that seemed to be looking beyond her ; then, as he became conscious of her words, he smiled and pressed her hand.

"You little goose," he said. "Did you really think that I should have minded ? You're mine now, whatever Sam McCorquodale may do."

It was too late for Inspector Dobson to start on his new line that night—too late even to talk it over with Superintendent Fraser. He wanted to get on to it afresh, and to devote his whole attention to following it up, though as yet it was mere guesswork to suppose that it would lead him anywhere. It was with great irritation, therefore, that he remembered that the inquest was to take place the following morning. The enquiry was most unlikely to reveal anything that he did not already know ; it would certainly be adjourned for a week or more, and the greater part of a day of his valuable time would be wasted by his enforced attendance thereat.

It was after four o'clock on the following day, Friday, October 31st, when the inspector was free—the inquest having been adjourned, at the request of the police, for a week. Within twenty minutes of the Coroner's rising, the detective was handing to a clerk in Mr. Samuel McCorquodale's office his official card, with the words

" *Re* Sir John Smethurst " written across it. The financier received him at once and waved him genially to a chair.

" Good afternoon, Inspector," he said. " This is an unexpected pleasure. I only wish your visit was not connected with such a bad business. A fine man, Sir John —a self-made man, but one of Nature's gentlemen."

" Quite so, sir. I understood that you were one of his greatest friends, and that was why I came to see you. I thought you might be able to help me about the financial side of Sir John's life. It's often a help to get an outside point of view—outside his office, you know, where the trees may have hidden the wood." The Inspector drew from his pocket the list of Sir John's undertakings. " Now here's a list . . ."

McCorquodale interrupted him with a laugh. " Not a bit of good coming to me, Inspector," he said, waving the paper away. " Smethurst and I were friends, yes— personal friends—but we were also enemies. The last person he would have confided in on such a matter was myself—one of his greatest rivals. It's best to be frank with you—I can't help you in that way at all."

The detective rose slowly to his feet, returning his rejected list to his pocket. He was rather taken aback by the firmness of the refusal. McCorquodale probably noticed this and repeated his apology.

" I'm really sorry, Inspector," he said, " but it would be wasting your time and mine if I were to pretend to a knowledge that I haven't got. As a matter of fact, you could tell me a good deal that I'd like to know, but I don't suppose that's what you've come here for. Have a cigar, anyway—or a cigarette if you prefer it." He pushed a heavy silver box across the table.

A flicker passed across Inspector Dobson's inexpressive face.

" Thank you, sir," he said. " I'll take a cigarette if I

may. It's good of you to be so frank with me; I'm sorry to have troubled you."

As the junior clerk, who was showing him out, pressed the bell of the elevator, Inspector Dobson said to him:

" By the way, Mr. Hoylow's not your chief clerk here still, is he ? "

" No," said the young clerk. " Mr. Sneddle's been chief clerk ever since I've been here—a year last August, that is."

" Sneddle ? Sneddle ? I seem to know the name." The inspector frowned, as if wracking his memory. " Is he a tall chap with a black moustache and glasses ? "

" Oh, no. He's quite small—clean shaven. He does wear glasses, though."

" Ah, can't be the chap I was thinking of. Hullo, here's the lift. Well, thanks. 'Evening."

Stepping out of the lift on the ground floor, the inspector turned aside into a little recess in the hall and drew from his breast-pocket a gun-metal cigarette-case. In the case was a partly smoked cigarette, marked in gold with a Turkish hieroglyphic. It was the cigarette end which he had found in the ash-tray on the dead man's writing-table.

Taking from his lips the cigarette which Mr. McCorquodale had given him five minutes ago, the inspector examined the marking on it. It also showed a Turkish hieroglyphic. He put the two side by side and compared them. They were identical.

CHAPTER XVIII

AN OLD ACQUAINTANCE

INSPECTOR DOBSON was delighted with his good fortune in the matter of the cigarette; his bad start on the fresh scent had been fully retrieved. He had a good knowledge of cigarette markings, and he believed that this was a Turkish brand which did not come on to the English market—that it was, in other words, supplied to its purchaser direct from Turkey. If this were so—and it could easily be confirmed—there was a strong presumption that McCorquodale was the only man in London who smoked this brand of cigarette, and the fact that one of them had been smoked in the murdered man's study on the night o the murder was, to say the least of it, suggestive.

Putting the two ends together in the gun-metal case, and returning it to his pocket, the inspector left the building and turned up the street in the direction of the Mansion House. Crossing over a hundred yards up, he walked back on the opposite side until he was nearly opposite the doorway he had just left. Then, buying an evening paper, he stood aside in an alley-way and became apparently absorbed in its contents. His patience was not unduly strained ; within twenty minutes he saw emerge from the doorway opposite a man who answered the description which the young clerk had given of his chief. The man turned in the direction of the Mansion House and the inspector followed, the crowd making it a simple matter for him to keep at the heels of his quarry without attracting his attention. Before long, however, the man turned down an alley which at the moment was deserted. The inspector at once quickened his pace and touched the other on the shoulder.

" Just one moment, Mr. Sneddle," he said.

Mr. Sneddle stopped abruptly. Inspector Dobson thrust into his hand his official card. As his eye fell upon it, Mr. McCorquodale's chief clerk turned slowly white.

" What—what is it ? " he said. " What do you want ? "

The inspector had already summed up his man and settled on his line of action.

" Just want a quiet word with you, Mr. Sneddle," he

said. " There's a little place round the corner where we can get a cup of tea or a glass—whichever you prefer."

It did not appear to enter into Mr. Sneddle's head to refuse. Within three minutes the two men were seated in a small room with two glasses of port beside them. The inspector turned towards Mr. Sneddle, and as he did so, he was struck by something familiar in the latter's face. He put down the glass which he was raising to his lips.

" Have we met before ? " he said. " I seem to know your face."

" I don't think so," replied Mr. Sneddle. " Where should we have met ? I certainly don't know you."

" Well, that's odd. I felt sure I knew your face." The inspector continued to gaze at Mr. Sneddle. Mr. Sneddle evidently did not like being gazed at. He fidgeted.

" What is it you want ? " he said. " Why have you brought me here ? "

Mr. Dobson desisted from his inspection and turned his attention to the business of the moment. " I just want a little information from you, Mr. Sneddle," he said. " We have reason to believe that your employer was engaged upon some financial transactions which were in some way connected with the late Sir John Smethurst. I have been to see Mr. McCorquodale this morning, but could learn nothing from him. We intend, however, to have that information, and as you are probably, after your employer, the person best fitted to give it to us, it is your duty to do so. What we want to know is this : Was Mr. McCorquodale engaged on some operation in which Sir John Smethurst figures as a rival, and if so, what are the details of that operation ? "

As he talked the detective was surprised to see the look of anxiety gradually leave Mr. Sneddle's face; and in its place appear one of confidence and even contempt. As the inspector finished, the chief clerk rose abruptly from his chair.

"What the devil do you mean by trying to pump me about my employer?" he said harshly. "You know absolutely nothing at all. And you can go straight to hell."

The astonished detective sat back gazing at this rampant worm with his mouth open. Mr. Sneddle turned towards the door. As he did so, some movement of his—perhaps a twist of the shoulder—flashed into the inspector's brain the picture that he had been trying to recall.

He sat up abruptly, and as Mr. Sneddle's hand touched the door-knob, he spoke :

"Just a moment, William Lathurst," he said.

*   *   *   *   *

At a quarter to seven that night Inspector Dobson walked into Superintendent Fraser's room at Scotland Yard. He was plainly bursting with intelligence—or perhaps " information " would be a less misleading word.

"Ah, there you are," said the superintendent. "You look as if you'd got it in your pocket this time. 'Bout time, too."

The detective looked bewildered. "Got what, sir?" he said.

"Well, the weapon, or the murderer, or the missing will, or something."

Inspector Dobson's face brightened. "Is there a missing will, sir?" he asked eagerly.

The superintendent looked at him sadly. "I'm afraid there's something missing," he said. "Anyway, what have you got up your sleeve?"

This time the inspector's sense of humour did not let him down.

"Not the weapon, I'm afraid, sir," he said. "But things are moving now. I'm on the right track now, I think. You haven't heard about it yet. I only got on to it late last night."

He proceeded to tell his chief what he had learnt the

previous evening about Samuel McCorquodale, about his interview with the latter, and, finally, about his interview with Mr. Sneddle, McCorquodale's chief clerk.

"I had a wonderful piece of luck there," he said. "Directly I spoke to the fellow I felt he'd got an uneasy conscience, and then I thought I'd seen him before somewhere. Then when he turned to leave me, I saw the whole picture—he was turning to leave the dock after getting seven years for forgery. That was ten years ago—I'd had a small hand in the case. He'd done his time, but he'd started again with forged references. That's how I got him to talk—he knew he'd lose his job, and probably any chance of another, if this came out. He told me exactly what I wanted to know. McCorquodale's been trying to get a concession in Brazil for electrifying railways —two of the principal ones connecting Rio with the interior. He knew he was up against another big man, but he had good reason for supposing he was going to get it. Then, ten days ago, a letter came that knocked him all into a heap. This chap Sneddle, or Lathurst, or whatever his real name is, got a look at it afterwards, and it was a letter from the Brazilian Government telling McCorquodale that the concession had been granted to Smethurst. Sneddle says it knocked him right out for a day or two ; he thinks McCorquodale has dropped a packet over it—been speculating on his chances, or something."

"Got the letter ? " grunted the superintendent.

"No, but Sneddle thinks he may be able to get it. Anyway, if it's what he says, it's a pretty complete motive."

"Why ? "

"Because with Smethurst out of the way the concession would almost certainly go to McCorquodale."

"Not it. His heir or his executors or his company, or whatever it is, would carry on just the same as if he were alive."

" No, sir. Sneddle explained that to me. The concession was not made to any company—not to the engineering company that would do the work—but to the financier, Smethurst, in person. He would carry out the work with the company that he was financing, but the concession was made to him personally. Sneddle thought his personal reputation got it for him, in front of men, including McCorquodale, who were bidding higher. Anyhow, with his death, the concession becomes null and void."

" Oh," said the superintendent, " that alters it. Now shut up." He sat back in his chair and shut his eyes. The inspector sat like a mouse, not daring to speak. At the end of twenty minutes the superintendent came to life again.

" Let's get it down on paper, Dobson," he said. " Check me if I'm wrong. Ready? Go ahead, then. M. has reason to get rid of S. On Monday night he finds an opportunity to return to S.'s house at midnight with S.'s daughter. He says good night to her and goes out, slamming the door, but, having latched back the catch while her back is turned, he is able to re-enter the house. He walks into S.'s study and tells him that he has brought his daughter back from the play. Having heard voices, but no words, in the hall, S. has no reason to doubt this. The slam might only have meant that the door was not properly fastened before. They talk and M. smokes a cigarette—one of his own brand—his first mistake. M. takes an opportunity to hit S. on the head from behind—probably S. was sitting at his writing-table, and M. may have leant over his shoulder to point out something in that financial paper. (You must find that weapon, Dobson.) M. then arranges the body, and the window, and the keys, and the gravel, to fit the story of someone coming in through the window. He does not notice that the telephone has been knocked over. He takes the memorandum-book—probably because it has information in it that he wants for his own operations.

Then he walks out, either by the front door, releasing the catch—no, that won't do, he would have to slam it. He walks out by the window and the garden. Walks home or drives—you must check his return, Dobson. What do you think of the story ? Does it fit ? "

" What about the scullery window, sir, and the flower-bed ? "

" H'm. Yes ; I had forgotten them. Probably he was being a bit too clever—wanted two strings to his bow. The objection applies to anyone who cooked that study window scene."

" You think it was cooked, sir ? "

" Must have been. You yourself found it was impossible to fall anywhere near the chalk outline without seeing the chap come out from behind the window curtain. Therefore it was impossible for Smethurst to have been killed in that way—at least, he might have been killed, but he would have half turned round and got the blow on the side or front of the head. No, there was some faking of some kind there."

" There's that quarrel that Mr. Hastings had with Sir John," said the inspector meditatively. " That looked very promising. I'm sorry to have to scrap Wollop's evidence, sir."

" Why scrap it ? You tell me this chap McCorquodale is quite a young fellow. Wollop's story may apply equally well to him. We know he was after Smethurst's daughter. Why, see here—wasn't Smethurst in trouble—financially, I mean ? Well, then—McCorquodale finds out about that and comes along with an offer to help in return for the old man's daughter. The old man stands up to him—that's the explanation of Wollop's story, you can bet, Inspector. Get that down in writing."

" Now, then," he continued when the inspector had finished. " You must tackle this chap again to-morrow. Get his story of what happened at the house and make him account for every minute afterwards—up to at least one o'clock. No nonsense, mind."

"No, sir," said Inspector Dobson. "There won't be any nonsense coming from him to-morrow."

"Well, good night, then, Dobson. Oh, by the way, you'd better let your friend Hastings—and his attractive young woman "—(the superintendent grinned sardonically) —" know that Captain Buby has confirmed his being at the Blue Stocking from 11.15 to 1 a.m. on Monday night."

CHAPTER XIX

CLOSING IN

INSPECTOR DOBSON'S eagerness to follow up his new trail took him into the city at an altogether unreasonable hour the next morning. Fortunately for him, Mr. Samuel McCorquodale was one of the early-bird type of financiers— and one, moreover, who did not begin his week-end on a Friday. At half-past ten the detective was again presenting his card at the office in Cornhill. His reception, however, was distinctly less cordial than on the previous day. The clerk returned with the information that Mr. McCorquodale was engaged, and had nothing to add to what he had already said. The inspector's reply was equally curt, and he himself followed on the heels of the bearer of it.

Mr. McCorquodale greeted him with a glare.

"What the devil d'you want?" he said. "I sent out to say that I was engaged. I told you yesterday I couldn't help you."

"You can help me a good deal, I fancy, sir," the inspector replied coolly. "I want to know all about Monday night."

"Monday night?" Mr. McCorquodale's heavy face reddened. "What do you mean, Monday night?"

" What I say, sir. You were at Sir John Smethurst's house that night, and my instructions are to get your account of your movements, and to ascertain why you have suppressed this important evidence up to now."

" I have suppressed nothing. I've been asked nothing, except for information about Smethurst's affairs that any child would know I couldn't give."

" Well, we'll leave that for the moment, sir. Now will you please tell me exactly what your movements were from the moment of your arriving at St. Margaret's Lodge with Miss Smethurst on Monday night ? "

Mr. McCorquodale sprang to his feet. " I'm damned if I do," he cried. " What the devil do you mean by cross-examining me like this ? It's a gross piece of impertinence —I shall report it to the Home Secretary."

Inspector Dobson was quite unmoved.

" Now look here, sir," he said. " If you take my advice, you'll quiet down and give me the information I want. Otherwise you'll have to come with me to Scotland Yard and give it there."

Calmly as he spoke, there was no mistaking his determination to carry his threat into effect. McCorquodale continued to splutter for a time, but at last he sat down again and, with a very bad grace, proceeded to tell his story. It was quite short and entirely uninforming. He had said good night to Miss Smethurst exactly as she had described, had gone straight out of the house, shutting the door after him, and after walking some distance had picked up a taxi and driven straight to his rooms at the Albany.

" I take it then, sir," said the inspector, " that after going out of the front door, you did not re-enter the house ? "

" No, of course I didn't. Why should I ? "

" And you didn't see anyone about—anyone, that is, whom you might now connect with the murder ? "

" No. If I had, I should have informed the police."

"About this taxi, sir ; where did you pick it up—off the Blenheim Road stand ? "

"I don't know anything about Blenheim Road. I walked down Park Road and picked up a 'prowling' taxi near Clarence Gate."

"If I might ask, sir, why did you walk all that distance before taking a cab ? Was there no other about ? "

"I walked because I wanted to walk, and when I didn't want to walk any longer I took a taxi. Is there any crime in that ? "

The inspector ignored this sarcasm.

"And you got to the Albany at—could you give me an idea of the time, sir ? "

"I don't know in the least. Some time after twelve, I suppose."

"Would anyone at the Albany be able to fix the time, sir ? The hall porter, or your servant—did either of them see you come in ? "

"My valet certainly wouldn't. He doesn't live there—goes away after I've gone to dinner. The night porter might have seen me—he's generally in his box, but I can't remember whether he was that night."

"And you didn't go out again after entering the Albany ? Could anyone confirm that ? "

"I shouldn't think so. Nobody watches over me while I sleep."

"And the taxi, sir. You can't help me to trace it, I suppose ? "

"No, I can't. I didn't notice anything about it."

"Well, I must do my best to find him," said the detective, rising. He walked to the door, then turned sharply and shot out at McCorquodale : "And what about that quarrel you had with Sir John Smethurst in Regent's Park ? "

If he had hoped to startle McCorquodale into an admission, he was disappointed. The financier only stared at him.

" Quarrel with Smethurst ? Regent's Park ? What on earth are you talking about ? "

And the detective had to leave with nothing more revealing than a blank denial.

Outside the Exchange he bumped into Geoffrey Hastings. " Hullo," he said. " I've got some good news for you, Mr. Hastings."

Ten minutes' conversation with the detective sent Geoffrey to St. Margaret's Lodge with a beaming face. He found Emily and Rosamund just going in to luncheon, and a place was soon laid for him. For five or ten minutes the servants were fussing round the room, and he could not speak. But Emily's sharp eyes had noticed the change in him, and as soon as Jackson's stately figure had finally disappeared through the serving door, she turned to him with outstretched hand.

" Geof, darling, what is it ? I've not seen you look like that since it happened."

" Em, I feel an awful selfish swine, but I am rather bucked. It's all right about my alibi. Jim Buby has told the Scotch police that he can perfectly well remember my coming into the Club just after he got back from the Gaiety that night—a quarter-past eleven, he puts it at—and that we played bridge together right up to the time I left—one o'clock—that's already been fixed by the night porter. And what's more, I'd already got some jolly good evidence on that myself. I went round to the Club last night and saw the wine waiter who attends the card-room, and he can swear to my being there for a long time, and he's constantly in and out of the room. So that's all right."

Mr. Jackson, entering the room with the next course, was horrified to find his young mistress hugging her guest. Emily returned to her seat with a blush of shame upon her cheek, but a sparkle in her eye. Rosamund beamed upon the two alternatively. Another five minutes of enforced silence followed while the neglected chicken was removed and replaced by plums doomed to a like fate. Geoffrey had to answer a stream of questions. It was not till they got up to Emily's sitting-room that he told them of the case against Samuel McCorquodale. A chill fell upon their spirits as they listened to the story, given to Geoffrey by Inspector Dobson, of the tightening of the net round this wretched man.

" The trouble is," said Geoffrey gloomily, " I don't know whether I ought to help them or not. I do know something that might be of use to the police, but it's awful to think of helping to hang a man that one knows, even if one doesn't like him."

Geoffrey had not yet told Emily anything of McCorquodale's offer to him. When Emily spoke, he was glad that he had not done so. Her voice, usually so gentle, seemed to him to have taken on a harsh note, and her eyes were cold with anger.

" What does it matter whether we know him or like him or not ? " she said. " If he killed my father, I'll gladly help to hang him, and you must do the same, Geoffrey. Of course you must tell the police all you know. Tell them now. There's a telephone—on my writing-table. Ring up Scotland Yard and tell . . ."

She was interrupted by an exclamation from Rosamund Barretta, who had seized Geoffrey by the arm to hold him in his chair.

" No, Geoffrey, don't ! " she cried. " Emily, how can you speak like that ? It's horrible to hear you. Let the police do their own work—don't join the hunt after this wretched man. You'll regret it all your life if you do —you're not yourself now—think what your father would feel to see you like this—he would be miserable."

For a moment it looked as if a quarrel might flare up between the two women. Then the tension relaxed as Emily's natural affection for her friend overcame her half-hysterical passion.

"All right, Rosa," she said. "I suppose you're right. It goes against the grain, though, to sit still and let that horrible creature go about as if he had done nothing."

"It's not proved yet that he has done anything," said Geoffrey quietly.

The tension did not completely disappear until, by an inspiration of Geoffrey's, the three of them were packed tight into his little A.C. two-seater and bowling out of London by way of Hammersmith and Richmond Park. The freshness of the autumn afternoon, the smell of burning leaves in the park, the sight of the lovely fallow deer, and even of their fellow-beings enjoying their holiday, soon revived their spirits, and they had a lot of fun chaffing about Geoffrey's pseudo-bogus alibi. They went on by Kingston and Staines to Eton, where they took a young cousin of Geoffrey's out to tea. The atmosphere of Rowland's stuffy little back room, though itself anything but refreshing, was refreshingly different from the air of tragedy that three of them had been breathing during the past week. It was with lighter hearts than they had known for days that they drove back in the dusk by Slough and the Great West Road.

They had hardly got in when Geoffrey was called to the telephone. The voice of Inspector Dobson, now unpleasantly familiar, greeted him.

"Good things never come singly, sir," he said. "Your taxi-driver has just turned up. He remembers quite well your picking him up in Blenheim Road and his taking you to the Blue Stocking. He hasn't been long at the job, and he wasn't quite sure which the Club was—that's what made him remember it so well. Now I've got all my work to do again to find another taxi-driver—and this time (he muttered half to himself) I rather hope I shan't find him."

Geoffrey dined alone with Emily. Rosamund had gone and Mrs. Spurling, who made a point of being out when the Countess appeared, had not yet returned from a visit to an old friend at Wimbledon. The evening was the first really happy one that the two lovers had spent together since the tragedy, and it was with reluctance that they said good night. Geoffrey walked round to his flat in St. John's Road. To his surprise he found his servant waiting in for him.

" Hullo, Raggle," he said. " What keeps you here at this hour ? "

Raggle's air was mysterious. He closed the door and drew Geoffrey into his sitting-room.

" I didn't like to trouble you, sir, but I couldn't go to my rest without letting you know. There's been a gentleman here to see you this afternoon. I told him I didn't think you'd be in, but he said you was expecting him, and that he'd wait. Gave the name of Forester. I didn't quite like leaving him alone in here, and yet he seemed all right. I couldn't very well kick 'im out. So after he'd been in here ten minutes I came back quiet like and looked in. He was doing something with those war ' suvneers ' of yours, sir—I couldn't quite make out what, but he'd got that little life-preserver of yours—what you said you used in trench raids—in his hand. When he saw me he put it back and said he wouldn't wait any longer. Then he went out—and he gave me five bob, sir—there it is ; I don't want it if he's not straight."

Raggle looked at his master's face as he finished speaking. Geoffrey Hastings was staring at the wall over the mantel-piece where, among an assortment of bayonets, revolvers, bombs, and other war trophies, there hung a small steel life-preserver. His face was deathly pale.

" Who was this man ? What was he like ? "

" He was a very large gentleman, sir," said Raggle, " very large indeed."

THE PACK DIVIDES

CHAPTER XX

THE PACK DIVIDES

EVEN detectives generally get a rest on Sundays, and
Inspector Dobson saw no reason for making an exception
in this case. His mind, however, was never for long off
the problem, and it was almost with a feeling of relief that
he set to work upon it afresh on Monday morning. He set
in motion the machinery for tracing the taxicab that had
driven McCorquodale to the Albany; interviewed the
night porter at the Albany, and got from him a qualified
recollection of the return of that gentleman " something
after midnight " on Monday night; interviewed Mr.
Wollop, with negative results; obtained from Sneddle a
copy of the letter from the Brazilian Government; interviewed McCorquodale's banker and obtained a bewildering
crop of figures, that it would take an expert to sort; and at
six o'clock was back in Superintendent Fraser's office at
Scotland Yard.

To his surprise the superintendent appeared to pay but
little attention to his recital of the day's work. When it
was over there was silence for some minutes. Then the
superintendent emerged from his brown study.

" Dobson, I think you'll have to go to Scotland."

The inspector was flabbergasted.

" To Scotland, sir ? " he gasped.

" Yes, Scotland. Place where the whisky grows.
Incidentally, the place where Captain James Buby lives."

" But we've heard from him, sir. He confirmed Mr.
Hastings' story."

" I know he did. That's why you'll have to go and see
him. Look here, Dobson, there's something wrong about

123

that alibi, and I'm going to find out what it is. You say that Buby confirms Hastings' story, but the question is : Is Buby telling the truth ? Remember, he's a pal of Hastings', and there's been plenty of time for Hastings to write to him. He may be lying. You must go and find out whether he is—can't trust these Scotch police to find out."

" But, sir, there's a lot more evidence that confirms the story. You know we've found the taxi-driver who drove Hastings to the Club, and the night porter is quite certain about the time of his leaving. And on Saturday night Mr. Hastings told me he'd found a waiter that was in and out of the card-rooms constantly taking drinks, and he can swear that Hastings didn't leave in between times. He knows Mr. Hastings personally, and when he read about the murder he realized that it would affect him—that's how he's so sure of the date."

The superintendent frowned.

" That's awkward," he said ; " but there's a hole some-where. Look here, Dobson, I've been working on this a bit behind your back. I told you to let Hastings know about Buby's evidence because I wanted to put him off his guard, and I wanted you really to think he was cleared, because then your manner would satisfy him that you'd left his trail. But I've never been satisfied either with his alibi or with his denial of the quarrel. On Saturday I put a man on to watch him. He lunched at St. Margaret's Lodge and afterwards he went off in a two-seater with two women—Miss Smethurst and this Countess woman, I should judge from the description. I slipped round at once to his flat and said I'd got an appointment with him there and would wait for him. His man showed me into his sitting-room ; that connects with the bedroom, and I slipped in and found, as I expected, his dress clothes laid out on the bed. The man would lay them out early on a Saturday so as to get a long afternoon off. I turned the pockets of his jacket inside out and collected the dust and stuff in a bottle. It's not as clear as I'd hoped, but I feel pretty sure there's some sand or grit of some kind in it. The geological expert's got it under a microscope now."

The superintendent paused and wiped his forehead. For the first time since Inspector Dobson had known him, he was showing signs of excitement.

" That was one of the things I was looking for," he continued. " Then I started hunting for a weapon. I couldn't find anything in the bedroom—of course, I hadn't time to do more than a superficial search—but as soon as I got back into the sitting-room I saw what I was looking for. He's got a collection of war souvenirs hanging on the wall over the fireplace—bombs, pistols, field-glasses, and things. Among them was a life-preserver—a small thing made of steel—a damned handy little . weapon. Do you remember that the surgeon said ' Concentrated weight— something more like a heavy hammer or a burglar's life-preserver rather than a poker ' ? There was the very thing. And what's more, *there were no finger-prints on it.* There were prints—faint ones, it's true—on the bayonet and pistol next to it, but this thing was as clean and clear as a new pin. I'm certain it had been handled last by a man wearing a glove. Now, why should it have been, if not to hide finger-prints ? A clumsy mistake, but a very likely one. Unfortunately, the valet, or whatever he was, was a bit sharper than I expected, or it was a bit of bad luck—anyway, he looked in and saw me handling the thing. I rather lost my head, I'm afraid," went on the superintendent. " I ought to have taken it naturally and asked what the thing was for. But I got rather flustered and came away, leaving some rather feeble message. I gave the chap five bob, thinking it might shut his mouth—anything more would have made him suspicious. But I'm afraid he'll tell his master. Can't be helped now."

The superintendent paused to recover his breath.

Inspector Dobson hardly knew whether to be pleased at the discovery of these important clues or resent the implied falsity of his own line.

" That sounds all right, sir," he said grudgingly, " but it may be all wrong. The grit in the pockets may not come from gravel at all—or if it does, it may not have come from St. Margaret's Lodge. And there must be hundreds of trench weapons hanging up in London now. And surely a murderer wouldn't hang his weapon up for every-one to look at ! "

" No, he wouldn't. But if it was already hung up, he wouldn't dare to call attention to it by taking it down. Still, as you say, both those may be false clues. But I've done a bit more to-day. I've been into this young man's affairs pretty closely. You ought to have done it yourself before now, Dobson. He's been speculating heavily, and unless I'm much mistaken, he's up to his ears in debt. I haven't had time to go into them thoroughly yet—it's really an expert's job—but there are big cash drafts in and out of his accounts—mostly out. The fellow's in Queer Street, or I'm a Dutchman."

The inspector was considerably impressed by the know-ledge which his chief had attained in so short a time—he was even rather humbled by it. But he was not yet convinced.

" Even if he is in trouble," he objected, " why should he murder the old man ? He knew he was pretty nearly broke, and there's nothing coming to him from his death. And, besides, what about McCorquodale ? They can't both have killed him ! "

" Can't they ? Why not ? I admit I'm not sound on the motive yet, but it's there somewhere. And I'm going to find out the way through this alibi—and if I can't get through, I shall get round. It looks as if it was good up to one o'clock. And Dr. Blathermore gave half-past twelve as the outside limit. Then how—by Jove, Dobson, suppose

Blathermore's wrong! We've only his word for it—these doctors always like to pose as infallible, but I don't believe they are. How can we check him ? "

" Dr. Jeacocks examined the organs, sir. He might be able to."

" No, he's sure to back up Blathermore. I want an independent check, but I suppose it's too late to get it. Unless—didn't you say there was a civilian doctor there before you got there ? "

" Yes, sir ; Sir John's own man—Bryant, I think his name was."

" We must get hold of him, Dobson. Look him up—here, give me the telephone directory. Bryant—Bryant—here we are—Dr. James Bryant, Blenheim Road, St. John's Wood—that'll be the chap. Regent 1010." The superintendent pulled the telephone towards him. " Regent one oh, one oh, please, miss. . . . Hullo, that Dr. Bryant's house ? . . . Oh, that you, doctor ? This is Superintendent Fraser, Scotland Yard. It's about Sir John Smethurst. Could you possibly come down here and have a conference with us ? I don't want it known that the police are coming to you. We'll pay your taxi each way. Very good of you, doctor. Bring your notes, will you ? " He hung up the receiver. " He'll be here in twenty minutes," he said. " Meantime, tell me again about McCorquodale. Afraid I wasn't listening properly before. We may want him yet."

The inspector launched once more into an account of his doings, but he had barely got halfway when Dr. Bryant was announced.

" Now, what is it ? " he asked, after shaking hands with the two officials. " I take it you haven't dragged me all this way over some red-tape nonsense."

" We haven't, doctor. This is the point. The police surgeon has fixed certain limits of time between which the murder of Sir John Smethurst was committed. I want to check those limits. You saw the body before our doctor did. What is your opinion about the hour of death ? "

Dr. Bryant did not answer at once, and when he did it was with another question.

" Let me be quite clear what you want," he said. " Is it my personal opinion of the probable time, or do you want me to confirm the limits given by the police-surgeon ? "

" I should like both, doctor. But particularly I want to know how completely we ought to rely on our surgeon's limits. He places them very tight—a probable range of half an hour, with a possible margin half an hour either side of it."

"Rot ! " said Dr. Bryant brusquely. " I haven't made a thorough examination of the body, so I'd much rather not give an opinion of the actual time. But I've had enough experience to know that there is a very wide margin of possibility. A hundred factors may affect the condition of the body, especially after it's been dead five or six hours. I wouldn't tie myself down within three or four hours. I know it's the fashion in these police cases to be very precise and definite, but I've had thirty years' experience, most of it in a part of London where death is fairly common, and I know that precision is humbug."

" Then you think that it's possible the murder may have been committed after one o'clock—Dr. Blathermore puts it at between outside limits of eleven and twelve-thirty."

" My note at the time, Superintendent—mind you, I only made a superficial examination—is that death probably occurred about seven hours previously—that is to say, about midnight. But if I were in a witness-box I wouldn't take my oath to be certain within two hours either side of that."

The superintendent leaned forward.

" This is vitally important evidence, doctor," he said. " Up to now we have gone on our surgeon's report that death occurred between eleven and half-past twelve. The man we suspect has a watertight alibi over that period, but a very weak one—a very suspicious one—after 1 a.m.

According to your evidence, it is quite possible that the murder was committed after that hour?"

"Possible, yes, certainly. I should have thought earlier; but that is possible."

"You're prepared to say that on oath?"

"I am."

"Thank you, doctor; then I'm afraid you'll have to before long—this just about clinches it."

After Dr. Bryant had left, Inspector Dobson released the flood of objections which he had with difficulty been restraining.

"But, sir, what about the telephone call? You forget that that definitely fixed the time at 11.45. And McCorquodale? What about him? Surely he's the man we want. What's the motive with Hastings? Where——?"

"Keep your hair on, Dobson," interjected the superintendent coolly. "The telephone receiver may have been taken off intentionally by Smethurst, to prevent interruption. McCorquodale may have been there, and yet not have killed him. As for motive, I'll find one." He leant forward suddenly. "Look here, my lad, your money's on McCorquodale, I can see that. Well, follow him up. Mine's on Hastings, and I'll follow him. And I'll bet you a month's pay—mine against yours—that my man swings before yours does."

CHAPTER XXI

ARRESTED

IT was with redoubled vigour that Inspector Dobson picked up the trail again on Tuesday morning. He was considerably chagrined by the way in which Superintendent Fraser had used him practically as a decoy, as well as by the almost contemptuous manner in which, he considered, his work had been treated. He was, also, secretly rather humiliated by the rapid results which his superior officer had obtained without apparent effort. Finally, the rivalry which the superintendent had deliberately generated, with the rather revolting wager attached to it, acted as a fresh spur to the inspector's efforts.

He was convinced in his own mind that, in spite of the circumstantial evidence which the superintendent had collected against Hastings, McCorquodale was the real murderer. He had undoubtedly been within easy reach of the dead man within a few minutes of the time which was strongly indicated by the telephone clue. He had a powerful motive for getting Sir John out of the way. His manner, finally, was highly suspicious.

The detective's first move was to look in at Scotland Yard and inquire whether anything had been heard of McCorquodale's taxi-driver, but no news had yet come in. He then called at the Brazilian Legation and, sending in his official card, was greeted by an exquisitely dressed young diplomat who looked as if he ought to be making his fortune as a hero of the silent drama. The inspector felt at some disadvantage in an unaccustomed atmosphere.

" I've come to ask for some information, sir," he said, " regarding the murder of a financier, Sir John Smethurst, who is believed to have been negotiating a big concession with the Brazilian Government. We are anxious to obtain details of this transaction, as——"

" Ah, excuse," murmured the attaché. " Our commercial secretary will no doubt be able to help you. I will fetch him."

A few minutes later, a slightly older but no less exquisite hero appeared. He bowed to the inspector.

" Will you trouble yourself to step to my office ? " he said. " I have there papers." When they were in the small and rather untidy room that made but a poor setting for this human jewel, the latter continued : " We have news of this affair. Our Ministry of Interior—that deals with it—is anxious. It was an important concession, dealing with the electrification of two of the main State railways. The concession had actually just been granted to Sir John Smethurst, largely on our advice—we know he was, what you say, 'a straight one.' Now our Ministry ask what happen."

"Yes, sir, and that's just what I want to know. What happens next? Now that Sir John is dead, who gets the concession?"

"Mr. Macor—Macordale—I cannot pronounce—was the highest bidder. The Ministry cable to ask more about him—he will probably obtain. But we did not recommend him in the first place."

"Ah, that's just what I wanted. McCorquodale—that's the name, eh?—he will come in for the goods now. Or, rather, thinks he will," the inspector added under his breath.

Taking leave of his obliging informant, the inspector, encouraged by this early success, decided rather daringly to take a leaf straight out of the superintendent's book. He took a bus to the Albany, and entering it by the door in Piccadilly—on the previous day his dealings had been with the porter at the Burlington Gardens entrance—he made his way to the rooms occupied by Mr. Samuel McCorquodale. His ring was answered by a sharp-looking valet.

"Mr. McCorquodale in?" he asked.

"No, sir," replied the man. "Mr. McCorquodale is at his office—in the City, sir."

"But he told me to meet him here!" The inspector's voice suggested pained surprise. "Eleven-thirty sharp, he said—and it's now twenty-five to twelve."

"I think not, sir," said the valet. "It's only just the quarter by this hall clock, sir, and I set that every night by wireless."

"Well, by Jove! what's come to my watch?" ejaculated

the guileful inspector. " Well, that accounts for it. I'll just have to wait for him."

The valet led him through a tiny hall and opened the door of a large sitting-room, handsomely furnished in the style of Albert the Good.

" What name shall I tell Mr. McCorquodale when he comes in, sir ? " he inquired.

" Wollop," replied the detective, who was not of an inventive turn of mind. " Sir Herbert Wollop," he added, with a dash of imagination.

Having indicated to his titled visitor the cigars and an unlocked " tantalus," the valet withdrew. The detective cast a rapid glance round the room. The first object to catch his eyes—probably owing to its incongruity in the early Victorian setting—was a large photograph of Mr. Samuel McCorquodale himself, disguised as an officer of the Royal Naval Air Service. Inspector Dobson snorted.

" Nice sort of chap, hanging his own picture up," he said. " I bet his ' bit ' was driving admirals about in a Rolls-Royce."

He was about to investigate further, when he was startled to hear the sound of a voice in the hall. Could McCorquodale really have returned ? The detective tiptoed to the door and listened. At once his face cleared—he realized that the voice was only that of the valet telephoning. Then some words caught his ear, and a look of consternation came into his face. He had just time to jump away from the door and turn towards the window, when the former opened and the valet came in.

" Mr. McCorquodale's compliments, sir," he said politely, " and will Inspector Dobson kindly leave his rooms at his earliest convenience ? "

The inspector walked past the smirking valet and out of the flat with a disconcerted look on his face. But in his pocket there reposed an excellent likeness of Mr. Samuel McCorquodale.

" That may come in useful for identification," he said to himself, by way of consolation.

He might, of course, have got a search warrant that would have given him free access to McCorquodale's rooms, but, before applying such drastic measures, the inspector thought he would try and persuade McCorquodale to give him the permission that he wanted. He took a bus to the Mansion House, and was soon at the door of the big Cornhill building which housed, among many others, Mr. Samuel McCorquodale and his schemes. As he walked up the steps, a young man emerged from the building whose face was vaguely familiar to him. The detective stopped for a minute and watched the young man disappear in the crowd, trying to recall where he had seen him before. The memory, however, escaped him, and it was not till he was ringing the bell of McCorquodale's office on the second floor that it flashed across him that it was the Smethursts' footman, James Riley, that he had seen. No doubt the absence of livery had hindered his recognition.

The inspector was puzzled to know what could have brought Riley here—presumably to see McCorquodale—in plain clothes, and at this hour of the day. A possible explanation crossed his mind.

" I wonder," he said to himself. " Can it be blackmail ? Did he see McCorquodale that night ? It's quite on the cards."

It was too late to follow Riley now, but there would be no difficulty about getting a word with him at St. Margaret's Lodge.

The inspector was greeted with a variation of the usual formula. Mr. McCorquodale was engaged but would see him in five minutes. He waited patiently, and at the end of ten minutes asked the clerk to let Mr. McCorquodale know that his business was urgent and that he would like an immediate interview. The clerk came back at once and announced that, much to his surprise, Mr. McCorquodale's room was empty. He must have forgotten or else received some urgent summons, and gone out by his private door which opened directly on to the landing. The detective cursed his own stupidity.

" The cunning fox," he said to himself. " He didn't want to face another talk. I shan't find him now. I shall have to get that search warrant."

Before going back to the Yard, however, the inspector thought it would be well worth his while to pay a visit to St. Margaret's Lodge, and try to find out what connection Mr. James Riley had with Mr. Samuel McCorquodale. He took the Inner Circle to Baker Street and decided to complete the journey on foot, in order to time the walk from Clarence Gate, where McCorquodale said he had picked up a cab, to St. Margaret's Lodge. Strolling at an easy pace, the inspector found that it took him twelve minutes.

At St. Margaret's Lodge, however, he drew blank. A strange footman opened the door, and Mr. Jackson, on being summoned, told him that Riley had left three days ago at a few hours' notice.

" Said his sister was ill," said the butler with a sniff. " I always thought that chap was a wrong 'un—but, still, *honest soit qui mal y pense*, I suppose."

The news troubled Inspector Dobson. He felt that he had not given this young man the attention that he deserved. On his return to Scotland Yard, however, the matter was driven entirely out of his head by the news that a taxi-driver had just come in who thought that he was the man for whom inquiries were being made. The inspector found the man, one Albert Chucher, in the yard with his cab. He was young and intelligent-looking, and the detective was very hopeful of getting some valuable information.

" Yes, sir," he said ; " I think the fare I drove from Clarence Gate last Monday night must be the one you mean. But I didn't drive him to the Albany, though. That's why I didn't catch on at first that he was the one

I'd driven; but then when I began to think about it, it wasn't so likely that there'd be many gentlemen in evening clothes in Park Road at midnight on the same night. So I came along. It wasn't to the Albany I drove him, but to Black's Club, in St. James' Street. He was a bit odd—that's what made me remember him. When I picked him up he was walking in the roadway—not on the pavement—and though he was looking in front of him he didn't seem to see where he was going. I believe he'd have walked right into me if I hadn't blown my horn. That seemed to wake him up, and he looked round, as if to see where he was, and then hailed me, just as I was driving on."

"What time was this, Chucher?" asked the detective.

"It was a little after twelve, sir. Five or ten past, I should say."

"*After* twelve? Are you sure of that?"

"Quite sure, sir. Midnight's a time you notice in London. It's fairly quiet by then, and all the clocks striking together make a pretty good noise. Oh yes, it was after twelve."

The detective turned up his notes. He found that Miss Smethurst had put the time of McCorquodale's leaving the house at "about half-past eleven." He had unfortunately not got McCorquodale's own statement on that point, but Miss Smethurst had been fairly definite. If, then, McCorquodale had left the house at approximately half-past eleven, according to the inspector's calculation, made that afternoon, of the time it would take to walk to Clarence Gate, he should have been there long before twelve—probably at a quarter to. On the other hand, if, as the inspector believed, McCorquodale had gone back into the house and killed Smethurst at 11.45—the time suggested by the telephone call—there would have been just time for him to have arranged the body and the room as they had been found, and to have got to Clarence Gate by about ten minutes past twelve. The point was of great

135

importance, and pointed strongly to the guilt of McCorquodale. The fact that Chucher's fare had been apparently so perturbed as to walk in the roadway without looking where he was going, pointed in the same direction.

" Did you notice anything else about him ? " asked the inspector eagerly. " Was he dishevelled at all—look as if he had been having a rough-and-tumble ? "

" No, sir. I can't say he did that. But this might interest you—I found it in my cab next morning."

Chucher drew from his pocket a small paper parcel and handed it to the detective. The latter opened it and disclosed a white handkerchief. It was of good linen, unmarked, and was practically clean, except for one thick smear of blood.

" By God, that settles it ! " cried the detective, moved beyond his wont. " Look here, Chucher, would you know the chap if you saw him ? "

" I think so, sir," replied the young taxi-driver.

The inspector suddenly remembered the photograph in his pocket. He drew it out and thrust it into the other's hand.

" Is that anything like him ? "

Chucher examined the photograph carefully.

" Well, of course, he wasn't dressed quite so much the hero," he said, " but I should say that that was him."

Two minutes later, having disposed of Chucher, Inspector Dobson marched triumphantly into Superintendent Fraser's office and slapped the photograph and handkerchief down on the latter's table.

" Well, sir," he said. " I think I've got him." The superintendent stared at him.

" Got whom ? " he said.

" That chap—McCorquodale."

The superintendent continued to stare, then leaned back in his chair and laughed.

" You're a thought late, Dobson," he said. " I've just arrested Hastings."

CHAPTER XXII

THE OLD BAILEY

THE case of Rex *v.* Hastings came up for trial at the Central Criminal Court—the new " Old Bailey "—early in December. The adjourned inquest and the hearing before the magistrate had revealed the broad outline of the case for the prosecution, but the line of defence had been revealed on neither of these occasions, so that the coming trial was awaited with more than ordinary interest by the general public, and this was further heightened by the unusual character of the *dramatis personæ*—the wealth and position of the victim, the popularity of the accused man, and the youth and charm of the girl who formed such a tragic link between them. It had leaked out, too, by now, that another well-known financier had been strongly suspected of the crime, and was, in fact, to be represented by counsel during the trial.

The case was to be heard by Mr. Justice Ballence, a judge of high reputation at the Bar, by reason of his know-ledge, wisdom, and human understanding, but, in that he eschewed print and confined his public activities to his work, almost unknown to the general public.

The Crown case was in the hands of the Attorney-General, Sir Horace Stille, supported by Mr. Deeping Waters, and Mr. Suckling, whilst Sir Edward Floodgate, K.C., Mr. Voyce, and Mr. Larner appeared for the defence. Sir Isaac Sharpe, K.C., held a watching brief for Mr. Samuel McCorquodale.

The Court was crowded to overflowing when his Lordship took his seat. Until the appearance of the prisoner, the interest of the general public centred upon the pale girl, dressed in black, who sat near the solicitors' table and gazed with anxious eyes at the empty dock. Though pale and anxious, however, Emily Smethurst showed no sign of shrinking from the ordeal before her—indeed, she appeared far less overwrought than did Rosamund Barretta, who sat beside her, and whose uneven breathing and restless hands revealed the depths of her sympathy for her two friends in the terrible trouble into which they had both been plunged. It was not long, however, before the general interest was switched to the dock itself, into which the accused man was ushered by two warders. Geoffrey Hastings also was pale, but there was a look of quiet confidence on his face and he exchanged a smile of greeting with Emily before turning to bow to the Judge. The jury—ten men and two women— were soon sworn, without any objection from the defence, and, in the absence of the Attorney-General, who was detained by a ministerial embarrassment, Mr. Deeping Waters rose to open the case for the Crown.

" Members of the jury," he said, " the story which I am about to unfold to you, and of the truth, or otherwise, of which you are the sole arbiters, will, I think, fill you first with amazement and then with horror to a degree which could never be aroused by deeds of far greater violence and bestiality committed by members of the criminal classes who more commonly appear within this court of justice. The young man who stands before you "—Mr. Waters pointed a dramatic finger at the dock—" charged with the terrible crime of murder, has enjoyed every advantage which money and the care of loving and thoughtful parents could provide—good education at the best schools and University, good health, warm friends, freedom from care, and a sufficiency of money to remove all possibility of hardship and temptation. Up to the time of the war there was no need, from a financial point of view, for this young man to enter the struggle for existence into which his less fortunate fellows are plunged at the moment of leaving their parents' roof. It is to his credit—and I say it willingly and unhesitatingly—that he did choose from the first to be a worker, rather than an idler—and so avoided the temptations, which, we are told, Satan provides for idle hands. The war came, and Geoffrey Hastings, at that time secretary to a prominent politician, at once threw up his billet and joined one of the most famous regiments in His Majesty's Army, served throughout the war with great distinction, was twice wounded, and gained the Military Cross. At the end of the war, after a short time of relaxation and travel, he was appointed secretary to one of the wealthiest and most influential men in the world of finance—Sir John Smethurst. Within a few years Hastings had won the entire confidence of his chief, and was entrusted with all the secrets of his great financial operations. Finally, no longer than a few months ago, he attained to the greatest treasure of all—the hand of his employer's only daughter and heiress. Could any young man's lot have fallen upon fairer ground? Could anyone have enjoyed more fully the advantages of that wonderful civilization which has brought us now to so great a distance from the brute creation, from which, if we are to believe the teachings of modern science, we are sprung. And yet now Sir John Smethurst lies in his grave, the victim of a brutal and treacherous attack, and his trusted secretary and chosen son-in-law stands in that dock accused of being the perpetrator of this loathsome crime."

Mr. Deeping Waters paused to observe the effect of his eloquent opening. The gratification which he gathered from the awed silence of the general public and the respectful attention of the jury was tempered by his observation of a slight frown upon the brow of his leader, who had come into court within the last few minutes. He resumed with slightly less gusto.

" I shall not comment now upon the horror of this tragic situation. I shall simply relate to you, in as few words as possible, the story of the last few months so far as it affects the case which you are here to try—merely reminding you that every word of this story can, and will, be attested by the evidence of unimpeachable witnesses.

" Sir John Smethurst was, as I have told you, one of the leading financiers of this country. Among many other activities, one of his principal lines of operation was to obtain a concession from some under-industrialized country for the sole right to carry out some big industrial undertaking, and then, having previously bought a controlling share in some genuine but not very flourishing business engaged in that particular industry, to employ it in the carrying out of the undertaking. Naturally, if the undertaking were a profitable one—and a man of Sir John's experience and ' flair ' would seldom be mistaken on that point—there would be considerable profits from that undertaking, and also—and this is a point to which I would draw your particular attention—the shares in that business— that company—bought by Sir John at a low figure owing to its not very flourishing condition, would soar up by reason of this successful undertaking to a high price at which they could be sold by Sir John, should he so decide, at a considerable profit.

" Coming from the general to the particular, about six months ago Sir John Smethurst entered into negotiations with the Brazilian Government for the sole right to electrify the State railways between Rio, the capital, and various important towns in the interior, intending, if successful, to employ on the carrying out thereof the West Lancashire Jubilee Engineering Company, a large firm of general and electrical engineers which, bearing a sound reputation before the war, had, owing to lack of enterprise in its control, since fallen rather into a back-water in the engineering world, its shares having fallen—its ordinary shares, that is to say—to the modest figure of 8s. 6d. At this figure Sir John had bought up two-thirds of the shares, which at the time were scarcely marketable and paying no dividend, so that the holders were delighted to be rid of them, and obtained thereby definite control of the business. He quietly brought about changes in the management and organization of the business so that it should be, when the time came, fully able to cope with the great undertaking he was purchasing for it. Now as to this undertaking, Sir John knew that there were rival suitors for the concessions in the field, and notably among them Mr. Samuel McCorquodale, of whom you will hear more, but he believed that his great reputation would obtain him the prize, even though others might bid higher for it. And, in fact, on Monday, October 27th last, there arrived in London—at Sir John's office in the City, in fact—by the late afternoon post, a communication from the Brazilian Government, informing Sir John that the concession had been granted to him. That letter was placed, as was the custom of the office with letters marked as confidential, in the basket of the secretary, Geoffrey Hastings, who, in the ordinary course, would look through them before taking them to his employer.

" Now let us turn for a moment to the affairs of this secretary. Since his return from the war, or rather, since his return from his post-war travels, Hastings has developed a taste for speculation. At first it took quite a modest form, and followed largely in the footsteps of his employer, who was not likely to lead him far astray. Latterly, however, Hastings has relied more and more upon his own judgment, and, operating in larger and larger figures, has on occasions gone counter to his employer's operations. That way, for the trusted confidant of a financial magnate, lies danger. Now, it had not escaped the notice of this astute young man that things had begun to go amiss with Sir John Smethurst's affairs. The Russian revolution, the fall of the mark, and all the upheavals of war and post-war finance, had reacted adversely upon Sir John. He was, to put it shortly, in difficulties—in fact, it may hardly be too much

141

to say that he was threatened with bankruptcy, though, being an indomitable and optimistic man, he would never admit it. But the astute secretary, noticing the trend of affairs, began, as I have said, to operate against his employer."

Sir Edward Floodgate rose abruptly to his feet.

" My Lord," he said. " I object to that expression. It is perfectly open to anyone, in however confidential a position, to buy or sell in the open market either in consonance with the operations of his principal or not. Such buying or selling can in no way be described as ' operating against ' the interests of an employer—it is merely an expression of personal opinion. To describe it as my learned friend has done is grossly misleading."

The Judge nodded.

" Thank you, Sir Edward," he said. " I was about to make an observation on the point myself, though I cannot go quite the whole way with you. Mr. Waters, I have allowed you considerable latitude, but I think you are inclined to draw rather too freely upon the generous sources of your eloquence. You should, I think, at this stage confine yourself more closely to bare facts. The expression to which the learned counsel has objected "—the Judge glanced at his notes—" ' the astute secretary began to operate against his employer,' suggests hostile action and is inclined to be misleading. I agree with you, however, that the practice of independent speculation by a confidential employé, though perfectly legitimate, is not altogether free from danger."

The learned Judge bowed to the learned counsel, who likewise bowed, murmuring " if your Ludship pleases." Similar bows were exchanged between his Lordship and Sir Edward Floodgate, and the case proceeded.

" At the time that Sir John Smethurst bought the bulk of the shares of the West Lancashire Jubilee Engineering Company, Hastings similarly bought a considerable block of the same shares—four thousand pounds' worth, I believe . . ."

Sir Edward was on his feet again.

" My Lord, I must protest again. My client bought four one-thousand pound shares at eight and sixpence each, at a cost, that is, of seventeen hundred pounds. The shares were worth seventeen hundred pounds, not four thousand pounds."

The Judge bowed again, and looked at Mr. Waters.

" My Lord, that is so. The nominal value of the shares was four thousand pounds ; the actual value, at the time, seventeen hundred pounds."

" We had better adhere to actuality, I think, Mr. Waters. Go on."

Blushing slightly, and murmuring the familiar formula, Mr. Waters continued :

" The very fact of purchase by a man of Sir John's prestige, gentlemen, enhanced the value of these shares, which, within a few weeks, advanced to ten shillings. Hastings, content, evidently, with a small quick profit, sold, obtaining for his four thousand shares the sum of two thousand pounds—a profit of three hundred pounds. With this two thousand pounds he bought a block a shares in Lacec Limited—the name is an abbreviation, I understand, of the London and Continental Engineering Company —the engineering concern controlled by Mr. Samuel McCorquodale, who, as I have told you, was the principal rival of Sir John Smethurst for the Rio railways concession. This transaction, mind you, was a genuine investment— Hastings bought and paid for these two thousand pounds' worth of shares in Lacec Limited.

" But there followed a transaction of a very different nature. Ten days before the date of the crime, acting either on his own judgment, or from supposedly ' inside ' information as to the recipient of the concession—I have no information as to that—Hastings' bought ' fourteen thousand pounds' worth of shares in Lacec Limited. But this time he did not pay for them with hard cash—he had not got fourteen thousand pounds; he arranged with his broker to ' carry ' them for his account, not intending to take them up, but hoping that the shares would boom almost at once and that he would be able to ' sell ' them again before the fortnightly ' settling ' or carrying ' over ' day. He was, in fact, being what the Stock Exchange call ' a bull.' My suggestion is that, believing that the Rio concession was about to be granted, not to his own employer, but to Mr. Samuel McCorquodale, he speculated heavily in the shares of the company—Lacec Limited—which he knew Mr. McCorquodale would employ upon the concession and whose shares would, directly the information became public, boom to such an extent that he would make a very large profit by selling them. At this point I should tell you that Hastings' previous speculations and extravagances—his banking account shows, among others, large cash payments, some, but not all, of which we have been able to trace—had landed him in a disastrous financial position. He was heavily in debt. He had borrowed from money-lenders, and, of course, if this last heavy speculation in Lacecs failed—that is to say, if Mr. McCorquodale did not obtain the Rio concession, when settling day arrived he would not be able to pay for the shares ; he would be forced to sell at a loss and would be completely ruined. He would lose his position and, in all probability, his fiancée, too.

" Realizing his position, then, you can imagine his feelings when, on the afternoon of Monday, October 27th, he opened a letter from the Brazilian Government, saying that the coveted concession had been granted, not, as he had confidently anticipated, to McCorquodale, but to his own employer. Here, in his hands, was the order for his own doom, inevitable, complete. But wait. Even now it might not be too late. The concession was granted, not to a company, but to an individual, to Sir John Smethurst. If anything were to happen to Sir John, the concession to him would become null and void, and would then almost certainly be granted to McCorquodale.

" Members of the jury, it is the contention of the prosecution that Hastings decided then and there that Sir John Smethurst should not have this concession, that he did not show the letter to Sir John though Sir John was in the office at the time, that he concealed the letter, either upon his own person or elsewhere, and that very night, after enjoying his employer's hospitality and going to his Club to create an alibi, he returned in the dead of night and murdered him."

CHAPTER XXIII

THE CROWN CASE

THE pause which Mr. Waters allowed himself at this point was undoubtedly effective. Though the case for the Crown was, in general, known, it had not hitherto been delivered with the full weight of forensic skill, and Mr. Deeping Waters, since, on his Lordship's advice, he had deserted eloquence for fact, had become distinctly impressive. An experienced judge of crowd psychology would have noticed that the sympathy of the public, hitherto undoubtedly favourable to the good-looking young man in the dock, had slightly chilled. Mr. Waters continued :

" The facts on which the Crown bases its case are as follows : At 4 p.m. on Monday, October 27th, the office boy at Sir John's office took the afternoon post to the chief clerk, who sorted it, and gave back to the office boy the ' confidential ' letters to be placed in the secretary's basket. Now, the office boy is by way of being a philatelist and he noticed on one of the envelopes a stamp which interested him—he believed it to be a Brazilian stamp, but he had no opportunity then to examine it closely. As soon, however, as the secretary had left—at 5.30 p.m., that is to say—the office boy returned to the secretary's room to look for the envelope on which was the interesting stamp. He could not find it, either in the wastepaper basket or elsewhere. He looked for it also in Sir John Smethurst's room—it was his duty to tidy up after his principals had left—but he did not find it there either. It is to be regretted that he looked through the correspondence on both the secretary's and Sir John's tables to see if there was a letter there to tell him what the stamp had been. He found nothing. Now, it is conceivable that the letter was locked up, but it is highly improbable that the envelope would have been locked up, too—letters are very seldom kept in their envelopes in business offices. It is even more improbable that had Hastings shown the letter to Sir John, nobody in the office would have heard anything about it. The bid for the concession was well known, and it was of such vital importance to Sir John in the precarious state of his affairs that he must, in all human probability, have shown some sign, either at the office or at his own home, of elation at the success of his venture. You will hear that members of his family and household had noticed a change in Sir John—a state of suppressed excitement during the last three months—that they even date it to a visit from a foreign gentleman, a Mr. Fernandez, who transpires to have been a representative of the Brazilian Ministry of the Interior. The butler will tell you that on the last two Mondays, the day on which the South American mail would be expected, Sir John had ordered him to get up a special bottle of port, evidently that he might celebrate the great news that he was expecting. Finally, we have Hastings' own statement to the police, on the morning that the crime was discovered, in which he says that the conversation on the previous night had been of no particular interest and in which, though referring specifically to artificial silk, he makes no mention whatever of the Rio concession.

"As I have said, Hastings dined with Sir John that night, and stayed with him till eleven o'clock. Then, having said good night to him in the presence of the butler, and having engaged the butler in conversation, probably to impress on his attention the fact that he was leaving the house, and having even deftly called the butler's attention to the time, Hastings did leave the house, picked up a taxi-cab in the next street, drove to his Club, and played bridge there till one o'clock—a time not at all in accordance with his usual habit—and next day was able to hand the police a list of witnesses to a complete alibi up to 1 a.m. on the 28th.

"But after 1 a.m. it is a very different story. According to Hastings, he strolled down to the Embankment, sat there for some time, and then walked home to his flat in St. John's Wood. It seems a curious performance for a man in his position. Nobody saw him, either on the Embankment or on the way home. But he was seen in St. John's Wood—at 2 a.m.—by a scavenger who happened to know him by sight. It is the contention of the prosecution, gentlemen, that the accused did not go to the Embankment at all, but that he returned to St. Margaret's Lodge—Sir John's house in St. John's Wood—entered the house by means of the scullery window, and, finding Sir John still in his study, murdered him by striking him on the back of the head with a small steel life-preserver. That he then arranged the room and the body—in a way which I will shortly describe to you—to suggest that Sir John had been walking in the garden and, leaving the window open, had given some intruder an opportunity to enter and conceal himself in the room, and then to kill Sir John on his return and attempt to rifle the safe. That is what, the prosecution contends, the accused wished to suggest, and after arranging that set-piece he returned to his own flat, being seen at a point mid-way between the two places at 2 a.m. by the scavenger to whom I have referred."

Mr. Waters then proceeded to describe the finding of the body, the appearance and arrangement of it and of the study, and the medical examination.

" It is a curious fact, gentlemen," he continued, " that the police-surgeon who examined the body at St. Margaret's Lodge, and who afterwards made the post-mortem examination, placed the limits of time within which death must have occurred at from 11 p.m. to 12.30 p.m. Those limits, rather arbitrarily fixed, if I may be allowed to say so, gave considerable difficulty to the police officers handling the case. It was only when they called in a second opinion that they found a way round the difficulty. The second opinion they obtained was that of Sir John's own doctor, who was called to the house directly the tragedy was discovered. Dr. Bryant made the first examination of all, though necessarily it was only a superficial one. He, while also suggesting midnight as the probable time of death, gave it as his definite opinion that it was impossible to fix the time accurately—he would not, himself, be certain within two hours on either side—that is to say, though believing death to have occurred about midnight, he considered that it may have occurred any time between 10 p.m. and 2 a.m. His opinion has since been confirmed by leading members of the profession, who will tell you that so many factors have to be taken into account when considering the length of time that life has been extinct that it is impossible to be certain within a considerable number of hours. The stiffening of the limbs and of the body generally —*rigor mortis* is, I believe, the professional phrase—begins very shortly after death, affecting first the extremities—the fingers and toes—and creeping gradually up the limbs to the body itself. But the pace at which this *rigor* comes on depends on a variety of things—on heat or cold, on the age of the victim, his general health, the state of his heart and organs, his general mode of life. So that where one body will be quite stiff within twelve hours, another may take twenty-four. Of course, in most cases a large number of these factors are known, or can be discovered, but that still leaves a wide margin for error.

"You will have the benefit of the evidence of several distinguished physicians, and from their evidence you will, I think, gather either that it is perfectly possible that the murder may have been committed any time up to 2 a.m. on the morning of October 28th. Now, between 1 and 2 a.m. on the morning of October 28th, Hastings tells us that he was sitting on the Embankment, or walking half across London—unseen by anybody, though he was a well-known figure in town. It is the contention of the prosecution, members of the jury, that between these hours Hastings was murdering the man who had given him almost more than a father could give—trust, affection, and, finally, his only daughter. He had, we know, a motive—a shameful motive; he had the opportunity; finally, gentlemen, he had, as you will hear, the very weapon with which expert medical opinion believes the murder to have been committed!"

On this dramatic note, Mr. Deeping Waters sat down.

After a short whispered colloquy with his leader, Mr. Suckling now rose to his feet.

"Call Alice Barsope," he said.

The head housemaid of St. Margaret's Lodge entered the box, and, having been sworn, was examined by Mr. Suckling as to the finding of the body, the state of the room, and kindred matters. At the close of the examination, Sir Edward Floodgate rose to his feet and smiled at the witness in the manner of an affectionate uncle.

"Tell me, Alice," he said, "who 'does' the study at St. Margaret's Lodge."

"I do, sir."

"And what time was it last ' done ' before the crime was discovered ? "

" Just before dinner on Monday night, sir."

" Did you empty all the ash-trays and clean up the grate then ? "

" Yes, sir."

" There is no possibility that an ash-tray—the one on Sir John's table, for instance—might have been overlooked ? "

" Oh, no, sir.   They were all done."

" Thank you, Alice, that will do."

There was no re-examination. Alice Barsope left the box and was succeeded by Mr. Henry Jackson.   The butler gave his account of the finding of the body, described the conditions and habits of life at St. Margaret's Lodge, so far as they might be thought to affect the problem, and gave his views on the restlessness noticeable in his master since the visit of " the South American gentleman " in July.   Finally, Sir Horace Stille, who had now taken over the conduct of the attack, drew from him a detailed account of the evening before the discovery of the body, eliciting the fact that no mention whatever had been made in his hearing of the Rio concession, and also a detailed résumé of the conversation he had had with the accused man wherein the latter, after saying good night to Sir John, had skilfully drawn the butler's attention to the exact time of his leaving the house.

In cross-examination, Sir Edward Floodgate extracted from Jackson his version of the " telephone clue," which had not so far been mentioned by the prosecution, and which now for the first time became known to the general public.   The butler described how his master had a private line, how the telephone on his writing-table had been found on its side with the receiver off, and how the telephone authorities had been able to fix the time of the unanswered call at 11.45 p.m.   The story made an obvious impression upon the jury.

Sir Edward then handed up to the witness a cigarette. "Do you know that brand of cigarette ? " he said.

"No, sir."

"It is a Beni Lukia—a special brand. Have you ever known your master to smoke one ? "

"No, sir."

"Or Mr. Hastings ? "

"No, sir. Not as far as I am aware."

Sir Edward closed impressively.

"Now, Jackson," he said. "You have, at the request of the prosecution, described in detail your conversation with Mr. Hastings on the night of the crime, just as he left the house. You must, during that conversation, have noticed him fairly closely. Did he give you the impression of being a man who had planned, and was in a short time going to commit, a dastardly murder upon his friend and benefactor ? "

"Indeed he did not, sir," replied the butler emphatically. "He looked as cheerful and pleasant as he always did, sir."

"You must often have seen your master and Mr. Hastings together. Was there any enmity between them ? "

"That there was not, sir. They loved each other like father and son."

"Thank you, Jackson."

The next witness was Dr. Bryant, who described, from the medical point of view, the finding of the body, and gave his views upon *rigor mortis* as outlined by Mr. Waters in his opening address. He was closely questioned on these views by Sir Edward Floodgate, who, though he could not shake him as to the wide margin of possibility, forced him to admit that the probable time of death was considerably before 1 a.m.

At this point the court adjourned for lunch.

CHAPTER XXIV

THE MISSING WITNESS

THE course of the cross-examination had already revealed the general line of defence—the probability that the murder was committed at a time when the accused was undoubtedly elsewhere. During the evidence of the next witness, however, the line was further defined from the general to the particular, and the reason for Sir Isaac Sharpe's presence became apparent. The next witness was, in fact, the key to the whole problem, providing, as he did, the bulk of the evidence from which both the prosecution and the defence drew their cases.

Detective-Inspector Dobson told the court of his appearance on the scene, of his detailed examination of the body and its surroundings, of his first impressions of the nature of the crime, and his subsequent discovery that many of these impressions were due to deliberate " faking "—the position of the body and the grit behind the curtain in particular. He told of the scratches on the latch of the scullery window, suggesting that that was the real means of entry. He told of his first conversation with the accused ; how the latter had made no mention whatever of the Rio concession, either when outlining his talk with Sir John on the previous night, or in subsequent conversation, not even when telling the inspector and Miss Smethurst about the precarious state of Sir John's affairs ; how he had suggested to the inspector the probability of Sir John having left the missing memorandum book in his desk at the office, whereas the chief clerk said that never during all his experience had he known Sir John to do so ; how, also, he had described his own movements on the night of the murder in such a way as to stress the period between eleven and one, for which he was able to prove an alibi, and to slur over the period between one and three, about which he could produce no witnesses at all.

Although Inspector Dobson had collected the bulk of the evidence for the prosecution, the greater part of it would be given by other witnesses. His examination, therefore, was not a long one. Sir Edward Floodgate rose to cross-examine. For fully a half minute he gazed meditatively at Inspector Dobson. The silence became oppressive ; the attention of the court was being deliberately concentrated on the coming question. Then :

" Inspector Dobson, you are the police-officer responsible, I believe, more than any other, for the investigation of this case. I want you to tell me—you are on oath, remember—whether in your heart of hearts you believe that Geoffrey Hastings killed his employer ? "

The eyes of the court turned upon the inspector. He reddened, stammered—but Sir Edward did not wait for an answer.

" I will put it to you another way," he said. Then he leant forward, and his next question seemed to flash across to the inspector with almost dynamic force :·

" In your opinion, who did kill John Smethurst ? "

There was an upheaval of black silk and white brief-papers as the Attorney-General sprang to his feet, but he was anticipated by the learned Judge.

" Don't answer that, officer," said his Lordship sharply. " Sir Edward, that is not a proper question. The inspector's opinion is not evidence. You are, of course, entitled to suggest an alternative explanation of the crime, but you must do it in a proper manner. Yes ? "

Sir Horace subsided into his seat. Sir Edward's bow hid a satisfied smile ; he had deliberately courted a snub in order to create an effect.

Bit by bit the inspector was forced to disclose the line

which he himself had been following during the latter part of his investigations. The telephone call, the Beni Lukia cigarette, his two conversations (" acting on information received ") with Mr. Samuel McCorquodale, indicated the general outline of the story, though much of it, as in the case for the prosecution, would have to be filled in by other witnesses—witnesses for the defence—Miss Smethurst, William Lathurst (*alias* Sneddle), and the taxi-driver, Chucher. Sir Isaac Sharpe, muzzled by the rules of procedure which allowed him no right of audience, was visibly perturbed, whilst the Attorney-General was more than once on his feet, but Sir Edward was keeping meticulously within the rules of evidence, and the learned Judge overruled all objections. The court was now keyed up to a great pitch of excitement, and was further regaled by the spectacle of one of the chief witnesses for the Crown being put through a hostile re-examination. Sir Horace Stille, however, was able in no way to shake the inspector's story. When Inspector Dobson left the box, the odds had swung right round again in favour of the accused.

They did not long remain in that quarter. The inspector was succeeded by Superintendent Fraser, who told of the finding of the life-preserver, unmarked by finger-prints, in Hastings' flat; by Hastings' own servant who, much against his will, proved that the life-preserver had, together with the other trophies, been cleaned by him shortly before the crime, and should, consequently, have borne his finger-prints; by Hastings' broker, who proved the transactions in which the former had been engaged; by his banker, who proved his banking account, and, incidentally, his precarious financial position; by Herbert Wollop, who told of the quarrel in Regent's Park. The superintendent, the man-servant, the broker, and the banker had suffered little at the hands of Sir Edward, but Mr. Wollop was forced to admit that the young man with whom Sir John had quarrelled might have been any one of some half a million young men of almost similar type in London. It was probably to reinforce the quarrel story that the Crown next called Sir John Smethurst's chief clerk. But to Mr. Waters' "Put up James Morrison," there was no response, and to the repeated cries of the ushers and police officials, through the court and the corridors: "James Morrison," "James Morrison," the echo came back "No reply," "No reply." Superintendent Fraser was seen to whisper to one of his subordinates, who left the court, evidently upon a mission of inquiry.

In default of Morrison, the box was next tenanted by a much more important witness—William Goke, office boy. William's story of the Brazilian stamp and the missing envelope was dramatically told and fully bore out the précis already given by Mr. Deeping Waters.

Sir Edward, rising to cross-examine, fixed the boy with a baleful stare.

"Goke. Where were you employed before coming to Sir John Smethurst?"

"With Petitt and Fogg, sir, solicitors."

"Why did you leave Petitt and Fogg?"

No answer.

"Were you discharged?"

A murmur: "Yes, sir."

"Were you discharged for stealing a postal order for 13s. 4d. from an envelope on your employer's table?"

William hung his head, but did not answer.

"Answer the question, Goke," said his Lordship sharply.

"Yes, sir," mumbled the unhappy William.

"And before that were you with Buckett and Buckett, bill-brokers?"

"Yes, sir."

"And were you dismissed from there for habitual lying?"

"Yes, sir."

Sir Edward sat down with a snort, and, despite the

efforts of Sir Horace Stille, William Goke, who had entered the witness-box and for minutes held the thrilled attention of the whole court, hero and cynosure of dazzled eyes, dragged himself out of it with heavy feet of clay.

Senor Juan de Fernandez, of the Brazilian Ministry of Interior, specially summoned from Rio de Janeiro, explained the terms of the concession to Sir John Smethurst, proved the despatch of the letter to Sir John by the mail which arrived in London on the afternoon of Monday, October 27th, and confirmed Mr. Waters' statement that, by reason of the death of Sir John, the concession to him became null and void.

Cross-examined, he stated that a letter had been sent by the same mail to each of the applicants for the concession, stating that it had been granted to Sir John Smethurst. He further agreed that, in all probability, the concession would now go to Mr. Samuel McCorquodale.

The dapper gentleman was succeeded by an unlovely individual of purple cheek and rheumy eye, who described himself as a street cleaner—Daniel Flush by name—employed by the St. Marylebone Borough Council. He stated that on the morning of Tuesday, October 28th, he had been working in the Blenheim Road when, at about two a.m., he saw " the gent. over there " coming from the direction of St. Margaret's Lodge. He knew the gent. well by sight, though not by name. He knew the time because, his being a lonesome job, he was given to listening for the clocks to strike. The clock had struck two either just before or just after he saw the gent. He could not remember anything special about the gent., except that he was in evening dress and looked rather rummy.

" Oh, you did notice something about him, then ? " said Sir Horace Stille sharply. " What do you mean by— ' rummy ' ? "

" Well, sir, 'e looked rather as if 'e might 'ave seen 'em."

" Seen what ? "

" Well, sir—the jim-jams, if you takes me."

Further examination by Sir Horace and, subsequently, cross-examination by Sir Edward, failed to elucidate in any way the appearance presented by " the gent." to the mind of Mr. Daniel Flush. Light, however, upon Mr. Flush himself was thrown by Sir Edward.

" Flush," he said, " are you an habitual drunkard ? "

On the objection of Sir Horace Stille, his Lordship came to the rescue of Mr. Flush's fair name. But Sir Edward stuck to his guns.

" I can prove it, my Lord," he said, and proceeded to draw from Mr. Flush damaging admissions, both as to his character in general, and as to his condition on the night in question in particular.

The last witness for the Crown was new to the general public, as his evidence had become available only after the case had been before the magistrate. Albert Boffin, dustman, also employed by the St. Marylebone Borough Council, deposed that on the morning of the Tuesday, October 28th, he had found in his cart a note-book, which he produced. A great many pages had been torn out of it, and only blanks left, but he had kept it because it had a good leather cover, and he thought it might come in useful for his son, who was a " scholard." He did not know from which particular bin the book had been tipped into his cart, but his route included Avenue Road (in which stood St. Margaret's Lodge) and St. John's Road (in which was the block of flats of which the prisoner occupied one).

Henry Jackson, recalled (Sir Horace explained that the point had not been put to him at his first examination as the last witness's evidence had, by permission, been added at the last moment to the depositions), identified the mutilated book as being his master's missing memorandum book.

With the closing of the case for the prosecution, the court rose. As Superintendent Fraser and Inspector

Dobson, not on the best of terms, emerged into Holborn, newsboys were distributing final editions. "Smethurst Case Sensation," "Missing Witness," ran the placards. They had just hailed a taxi when a young plain-clothes officer—the one whom the superintendent had despatched from court—hurried up to them.

"Just got you in time, sir," he said. "I went to Morrison's digs in Balham. They didn't know anything about him there—hadn't seen him since he came in last night. We went up to his room, and there he was hanging by his braces to a clothes-peg. Dead as mutton."

"Good Lord! suicide?"

"Yes, not a doubt of it—suicide."

CHAPTER XXV

THE CASE FOR THE DEFENCE

INVESTIGATIONS of James Morrison's affairs revealed the fact that, following his employer's operations with blind fidelity, he had invested all his savings in the West Lancashire Jubilee Engineering Company. The death of Sir John Smethurst, who was known to hold a controlling interest in the company, had caused a serious fall in its stock, and when the course of the hearing, before the magistrate in November, revealed, first, the reason for Sir John's purchase, and then the fact that the concession on which it was founded would now go elsewhere, the stock slumped altogether. Morrison might still have lived on his earnings if his employer had remained alive, but he must have known that at his age he could not hope to obtain elsewhere a salary half so generous as that which Sir John had paid him. He had evidently fallen gradually into despair, and had chosen the easy way out. Why he had chosen the opening day of the trial on which to kill himself was not clear, unless it was from an innate sense of the dramatic.

The sensation caused by the suicide of a witness was soon forgotten when Sir Edward Floodgate rose to open the case for the defence. In a quiet and dignified manner, much more effective than the fireworks for which he was more famous, Sir Edward explained to the jury that they need expect nothing dramatic—the accused man's defence was quite simple and, in his opinion, quite sufficient to acquit him of this terrible charge. It was simply this ; that all the weight of medical evidence, though some of it admitted the possibility of the time suggested by the Crown, pointed to the fact that the crime was committed long before Hastings left the Blue Stocking—up to which time his movements were fully accounted for by unimpeachable witnesses. The actual hour of the crime was, in fact, most strongly suggested, if not definitely proved, by the telephone call as to which two witnesses for the Crown had already spoken, and which would be further proved by officials of the telephone service. The Crown, suggesting that the crime was committed between 1 and 2 a.m., made great play of the fact that the prisoner was unable to produce any corroboration of his story as to his whereabouts at that time. But, as a matter of fact, it was probable that a man could sit for half an hour on the Embankment and then walk across London at that hour nine times out of ten without meeting with anyone who knew him by sight.

Further, it would be shown that much of the evidence brought by the Crown in proof of motive against Hastings told equally, if not more strongly, against a third party, and it would be proved that that third party had far greater opportunity for committing the crime than had Hastings, and had, indeed, actually been inside the house within a quarter of an hour of the time fixed by the telephone call.

It was not for him (Sir Edward) to conduct a case for the prosecution against this third party. . . .

"No, Sir Edward, it is not," interjected the Judge. "I am allowing you considerable latitude. Be very careful not to overstep the limit."

"If your Lordship pleases." Sir Edward did not for a moment suggest that this third party had committed the crime, but he was entitled to show that a great deal of the burden of proof brought against his client must fall equally upon the shoulders of another, and that his client's shoulders must therefore be relieved in at least an equal ratio. As to the story of Hastings having concealed from his employer the letter from Brazil granting him the Rio concession— and on this story the question of motive largely turned— it rested entirely on the evidence of a boy who had twice within the last six months been discharged for dishonesty. Mr. Hastings would tell the jury that in fact he did not receive that letter at all on Monday afternoon. It may have been put in his room, but he was with his employer all the later part of the afternoon and had left the office with Sir John by the latter's private door. He had found the letter in his basket when he got to the office on Tuesday morning, after the discovery of the murder.

The Crown had suggested, apparently as an alternative motive, that there had been a quarrel between Sir John and his secretary, but the only evidence they had been able to produce in support of this absurd story was that of a gardener in Regent's Park who was unable to give any idea of the date, and, though he was positive as to the identity of Sir John, admitted that he had seen no more of the second party to the quarrel than his back at a distance of a hundred yards—and that back, he had said in cross-examination, might have belonged to any one of a quarter of a million young men in London. On the other hand, they had heard the evidence of the butler, the trusted servant of over twenty years' standing, who stated most emphatically that there never had been any quarrel—that Sir John "loved Mr. Hastings like his own son." This would be corroborated by Sir John's own daughter, who believed implicitly in the innocence of her fiancé.

As to the suggestion that Hastings had in some way " betrayed " his employer by not following the latter in his financial operations, Sir Edward had never heard anything so ridiculous and even, in his opinion, improper. That an employé was bound to follow his employer on what he believed to be a road to ruin was an absurd suggestion. Hastings had inside information, and there was not the slightest reason why he should not use it to his own advantage, provided that his operations did not prejudice those of his employer—which, of course, they did not. It was true that Hastings had been in financial difficulties, and was still, but there was no crime—nor, indeed, any originality— in that.

Sir Edward submitted that there was really no case to go to the jury, but his client had expressed his desire, in any case, of going into the witness-box to tell his story, and he would, therefore, now call upon him to do so.

Geoffrey Hastings looked pale but very calm when he took his stand, accompanied by a warder, in the witness-box. There was nothing new in his story—its outline had already been given by his counsel—but his quiet, straight-forward manner made an obviously favourable impression on the jury. His ordeal came when Sir Horace Stille rose to cross-examine him. There was a cold contempt in Sir Horace's manner of addressing him that must have been very galling, and may have had some suggestive effect upon the minds of the more impressionable jurors. On that part of Geoffrey's story which dealt with the night of the murder, from the time of his dinner with Sir John to his return to his own flat, Sir Horace's attack made no impression. But when it came to the question of motive, the Attorney-General was more successful. For nearly an hour he plied the accused man with a pitiless interrogation on the subject of his financial operations, and forced him to admit that, though Sir John had taken him into his complete confidence as to his own doings, he had concealed from Sir John the fact that he was following a contrary course ; that Sir John would have been greatly disturbed had he known this ; that it was to his, Hastings', interest that Sir John's scheme should fail ; and that he had made no mention of the Rio concession, still less of the arrival of the letter, to Inspector Dobson, although it was obvious that the subject might be of vital importance.

Hastings was visibly shaken by the exposure of his undeniable deceit, and it was with less confidence that he met the Attorney-General's attack on the subject of the arrival of the Brazil letter. He still adhered to his story that he had not gone back into his own room, and that consequently he had not received the letter on Monday night, but he could give no explanation of why he had not done so.

" Surely," said Sir Horace, " you knew that Sir John was expecting—anxiously expecting—this letter from the Brazilian Government, and that Monday afternoon was the day on which it would most probably arrive ? "

" I knew he was expecting it ; yes."

" And yet you did not inquire whether the mail was in before you left the office ? "

" No."

" But did he not ask you whether the mail was in— whether the letter had come ? "

" I don't think so."

" I want a definite answer, please. You must know whether or not Sir John asked you a question of such vital importance. Did he, or did he not ? "

" No, he did not."

" Not even when you dined with him that night ? "

" No."

"And yet you have heard the butler say that on that and the previous Monday Sir John had ordered up a special bottle of port—the '96, I think he called it—as he thought you might be going to bring him some news that you and he might want to celebrate? Do you still say he did not ask you whether the letter had come?"

"I don't think so; we were talking mostly about the artificial silk trade."

Sir Horace threw down his brief with an angry gesture.

"Will you please answer my question. Did Sir John, or did he not, ask you about the Brazil letter on Monday night?"

"To the best of my recollection, he did not."

The Attorney-General stared incredulously at his victim, opened his mouth as if to ask him another question, and then shrugged his shoulders and passed on to the next point.

He questioned Hastings very closely about the life-preserver, in particular asking him for an explanation of the absence of finger-prints, in view of what his servant had said. The prisoner could offer no solution of the problem, unless it was that somebody wearing gloves had taken the weapon off the wall to examine it subsequently to the last time his servant had cleaned it. Asked for a list of his visitors since the date mentioned by the servant, he was unable to remember any by name, except his fiancée and Madame Barretta, and he agreed that if either of them had touched it they would have told him so. The impression made by this part of the cross-examination was so clearly unfavourable to the prisoner that the Attorney-General judged it good tactics to rest on his laurels, and he therefore intimated that his cross-examination was at an end. Sir Edward Floodgate did his best, by re-examination, to rehabilitate his client, but without marked success.

The subsequent witnesses for the defence had an easier time. Dr. Blathermore, the police-surgeon, and Dr.

Jeacocks, the Home Office pathologist, both gave it as their opinion that death had occurred prior to 1 a.m. on the 28th, though, under cross-examination, they both now reluctantly admitted that it was not absolutely certain. Emily Smethurst spoke of her father's affection for the accused man, and flatly scouted the idea of any quarrel between them. She asserted her complete faith in her fiancé's innocence. She was gently handled by Sir Horace Stille and yielded no ground to his suggestion that the quarrel might have taken place without her knowledge.

The only other witness of importance—a very unwilling one—was Mr. Samuel McCorquodale. Sir Edward Floodgate, without ever suggesting that the witness was the real murderer, succeeded in compelling his witness to tell of his share in the Rio concession transactions in such a way as to reveal the fact that the demise of Sir John Smethurst was at least as much to his interest as to that of the prisoner. His unsuccessful courtship of Miss Smethurst was also introduced under the pretext of its being a confirmation of the goodwill of Sir John Smethurst towards Geoffrey Hastings. The Judge disallowed, however, Sir Edward's attempt to extract the story of McCorquodale's movements on the night of the murder.

The close of the evidence for the defence was followed by Sir Edward's final address to the jury. The great advocate broke no new ground, but contented himself with a review of the evidence that had been given, both for the prosecution and for the defence. He pointed out that the evidence of Inspector Dobson, one of the chief witnesses for the Crown, quite clearly indicated a very luke-warm belief in the prisoner's guilt ; whilst two Crown servants engaged upon the case—the police-surgeon and the Home Office pathologist—had actually given evidence for the defence. He referred scathingly to the characters of two vital witnesses for the Crown, the office boy, Goke, and the scavenger, Fush. He compared with such witnesses the admirable character borne by the accused man, and emphasized the fact that his innocence was firmly believed in by two of the people most eager to discover the murderer of Sir John—his daughter and his faithful servant and friend, Jackson. Sir Edward's final peroration was in his most famous vein and moved the court so deeply that one of the jurywomen burst into tears.

The Attorney-General soon applied a cold douche of reason to the emotions awakened by his opponent. His address was really a résumé of that given at the opening of the case by his colleague, Mr. Deeping Waters, but he added to it a biting comment on the attempt of the defence to plant the guilt upon another man whose only sin was that he was a rival of Sir John Smethurst. Finally, he gave, in terms none the less damning for their moderation, his views upon the character of the prisoner, his financial operations, and his demeanour in the witness-box. In its different style, it was a speech no whit inferior to that of the eloquent Sir Edward.

The Judge deferred his summing-up until the next day.

CHAPTER XXVI

THE ELEVENTH HOUR

THE summing-up of Mr. Justice Ballence, although scrupulously fair, left little room for doubt as to his Lordship's own opinion. The learned Judge pointed out that it was no defence, in a case of murder, to show that another person had an equal motive and an equal—or even greater—opportunity of committing the crime ; the question for the jury to decide was whether or not the person now under trial committed it. The evidence against the accused man in this case was largely circumstantial, but then it nearly always was in cases of this description, for it was the rarest thing in the world for a murderer to be actually seen and recognized at his work. The present case turned largely upon the question of time. It had been suggested for the defence that the medical evidence tended to show that death must have occurred when the prisoner was indisputably elsewhere, but it was a matter of common knowledge that the symptoms—such as the degree of *rigor mortis* —upon which this opinion was based, varied considerably with each subject, and that it really was impossible to lay down an exact limit of time beyond any shadow of doubt. It seemed fairly clear that the period of time—1 a.m. to 2 a.m.—within which the prosecution said the crime was committed, was a possible time, and it was equally clear that the prisoner's account of his whereabouts during that period was extremely improbable, and was supported by no corroborative evidence whatever. It had been suggested for the defence that the actual time of the murder—11.45 p.m. —was fixed by a call which had been put through on the private line to Sir John's Smethurst's study by the telephone being knocked over by the fall of the body. As to that, the jury would form their own opinion, but to his Lordship there appeared little reliability in such evidence.

His Lordship proceeded to review the evidence of the various witnesses in some detail, drawing the attention of the jury to points which appeared to him of importance. Dealing with the question of the letter of the Brazilian Government, his Lordship suggested that the jury should ask themselves whether the lad Goke, even though his character for truthfulness was not irreproachable, would have been likely to invent the story of its arrival by the afternoon mail on the Monday and its subsequent disappearance. ❧ On the other hand, did they believe the story of the prisoner, who told them that Sir John Smethurst,

whose whole future turned upon that letter and who undoubtedly expected it to arrive that day, had not made any
inquiry at all as to whether it had arrived ?

After referring at some length to the evidence of Flush,
the scavenger, who testified to having seen the prisoner in
the neighbourhood of the crime at 2 a.m. on the day in
question, and dealing with the weapon, his Lordship proceeded to discuss the prisoner's financial operations, as to
which his views were not far removed from those of the
Attorney-General. Finally, he explained to the jury the
degree of certainty which was required to justify a conviction. It was not necessary for them to have absolute
and definite proof of every step in the case for the prosecution—what they did require was to be convinced beyond all
reasonable doubt—and by reasonable doubt he meant the
kind of doubt that a reasonable man might feel in the
ordinary transactions of his daily life. If they did feel
reasonable doubt, then the prisoner was entitled to the
benefit of it, and they should return a verdict of Not Guilty;
if they had no reasonable doubt, then, without shrinking
from the dreadful responsibility which it involved, it was
their duty to find the prisoner guilty.

There was a stir of suppressed excitement as the jury
retired, under the escort of their male and female bailiffs,
to consider their verdict, and as soon as his Lordship also
had retired the pent-up emotions were released in a buzz
of eager conversation.

Emily Smethurst leaned toward Sir Edward Floodgate.

" What do you think, Sir Edward ? I want to know the
truth."

Sir Edward looked steadily at her.

" It's no good filling you with false hope, Miss Smethurst,"
he said at last. " I am anxious—very anxious. His Lordship's summing up was definitely unfavourable. Mr.
Hastings' financial dealings have unquestionably told against
him especially by contrast with that poor chap Morrison's

tragedy. I think, too, that the jury believe Goke's story of the arrival of the letter. Of course, I may be wrong, and in any case there is always the Court of Appeal—but I am afraid the jury will convict."

A cry of anguish rang through the court, startling its occupants into instant silence. Every eye was turned upon the tall figure of a woman, who, with a look of utter terror in her eyes, was staring at Sir Edward Floodgate. Rosamund Barretta opened her mouth twice as if to speak, but when she did her words came in a scarcely audible whisper.

" Convict ? You said convict ? "

The distinguished King's Counsel was considerably taken aback by this dramatic reception of his confidential opinion.

" Really, madame," he said. " I must ask you to calm yourself. I gave that, as my personal opinion, to Miss Smethurst. I did not intend . . ."

Rosamund sank back into her chair and buried her face in her hands.

" Oh, my God ! " she moaned. " I can't bear it ! I can't bear it ! "

Emily, who had herself turned white at Sir Edward's words, was staring at her friend with a dawning bewilderment in her eyes.

" Rosa," she said. " Rosa, what . . .? "

But she got no further, for Rosamund again sprang to her feet, this time with grim determination on her face.

" I've got to tell it ! " she said hoarsely. " Sir Edward, you must bring them back ! I can't let him be convicted. I must tell them. I must tell them."

" Tell them what, madame ? " Sir Edward's curiosity was now fully aroused. " Tell them what ? "

" Where he was that night—after he left the Club ! He wasn't on the Embankment—he couldn't have been at St. Margaret's Lodge when they say he was—he was with me ! "

" With you ?   When ?   Till what hour ? "

" From about a quarter-past one till three."

" Till three !   But that's long past the farthest limit of possibility given by any of the medical witnesses ! "

" Yes, yes ; . don't you see ? "   Rosamund wrung her hands.   " He can't possibly have killed Sir John.   I could have saved him, but he wouldn't let me speak.   Oh, is it too late ?   Can't I speak now ? "

Sir Edward beckoned to Mr. Deeping Waters and the two entered a whispered colloquy.   Then Sir Edward turned again to Rosamund, and presently she was sitting beside him at the barrister's table, talking in a low voice, while Mr. Waters, on the other side of her, rapidly took down what she was saying.   After a time, Sir Edward rose and went across to the Attorney-General, with whom, after some minutes' consultation, he left the court.   Rosamund, after one nervous glance at her friend, remained at the barrister's table, her eyes downcast, her hands nervously plucking at a lace handkerchief.   Emily had not moved from her chair, but her body seemed to have shrunk into itself, her eyes, staring straight in front of her, were utterly expressionless.   All through the long ordeal of the trial her bearing had been full of courage and pride ;   now her world seemed to have fallen about her ;   her spirit was broken.

Presently the cry of an usher : " Silence ! "   " Silence ! " brought the whole court to its feet, and the Judge entered and took his seat.   The jury, looking puzzled, filed back into their box, and the prisoner, white and nervous, re-appeared in the dock.

As soon as silence was fully restored, his Lordship turned to the jury and addressed them :

" Members of the jury," he said.   " I have taken the almost unprecedented course of recalling you from the consideration of your verdict, because there has just been brought to my notice some fresh evidence of vital importance to the issue. The Attorney-General has very properly objected to the admission of further evidence at this stage because, he contends, the case is now closed. After the gravest consideration, however—grave, not only because of its effect upon this case, but because of the precedent it must create—I have reached the decision that, in the interest of justice—and justice is what I am here to see administered—I believe that you cannot arrive at a true verdict without hearing this evidence. I have therefore ruled, after hearing the arguments of counsel on both sides, that the case shall be reopened and that the evidence of this witness, who could, it is true, have spoken before, but who, for reasons which you will hear, did not do so, shall be heard. I fully realize, as I have said, the gravity of this decision, for which I accept, as I must do, the full responsibility. Call your witness, Sir Edward."

Sir Edward rose briskly to his feet.

" Countess Barretta," he said.

There was a stir of excitement as Rosamund took her stand in the witness-box and raised the Testament in her ungloved right hand. Her beauty was at any time liable to attract attention, but now the deathly pallor of her face, from which the dark eyes shone with almost unnatural lustre, combined with the mystery which surrounded her dramatic appearance to make the strongest possible appeal to the public interest. Before, however, Sir Edward could begin his examination, a further interruption occurred. The prisoner, who had looked bewildered when the Judge was addressing the jury, as soon as he heard Rosamund's name called had half risen from his seat, his hand stretched out to stop her. He sank back while the oath was being administered, but, as she turned towards the jury, he jumped to his feet.

" My Lord," he cried. " I have not asked for this witness to be called. I am perfectly satisfied with my trial—with my defence. I will accept the jury's verdict, whatever it is. I beg you, my Lord, not to let this lady be examined."

His Lordship leant forward.

" I appreciate your reason for making that appeal, Mr. Hastings," he said. " But I cannot accede to it. You did wrong in not calling this witness at the proper time, but in the interests of justice she must, in my judgment, be called now. That is my ruling, and I must adhere to it."

Geoffrey opened his mouth as if to make a further appeal, then sank back into his chair, and for the whole time that Rosamund was in the box, sat with his face buried in his hands.

Sir Edward turned again to the witness.

" You are the Countess Rosamund Barretta ? "

" Yes."

" Your husband was the Count Barretta, a Spanish subject, who was killed in the war ? "

" Yes."

" Where do you live ? "

" In Queen Anne Street, Westminster."

" Do you know the accused ? "

" Yes."

" What are the relations between you ? "

Rosamund's head dropped and her voice was hardly audible as she answered :

" He was my lover."

Again there was a stir through the court, but the interest was so intense that it was soon silenced.

" Do you remember the night of Monday, October 27th ? "

" I do."

" Please tell my lord and the jury what happened that night."

" I had dined alone in the restaurant attached to the Queen Anne flats, and sat up reading till late. At a quarter-past one Mr. Hastings came in. I had been expecting him. He stayed till three and then left. That is all I know."

" How do you know the times ? "

" I had expected him earlier, and I looked constantly at the clock. I had just looked, at a quarter-past one, when he came. I know it was three when he left, because we heard Big Ben strike as we said good-bye—he said he had not realized it was so late."

" Was anyone else in the flat who could confirm those times ? "

" Yes, my maid, Janet Kirby ; she let Mr. Hastings in."

" You are absolutely certain as to the date and the times ? "

" Absolutely."

" Why did you not give this evidence before ? "

" Because Mr. Hastings made me promise not to. He said he was absolutely certain of acquittal without my speaking. But when the jury went out to consider their verdict I couldn't bear it any longer." (This was a clever touch suggested previously by Sir Edward to conceal the fact of his own expressed opinion.)

The cross-examination by Sir Horace Stille revealed the whole sordid story of deceit and treachery in all its vileness. Hastings and Rosamund Barretta had been lovers before the former's engagement to Emily Smethurst. But they had no money—at least, not sufficient to satisfy their aspirations—and so it was arranged that Hastings, who then believed his employer's daughter to be heiress to a great fortune, should marry Emily, and that the guilty lovers should continue their intrigue surreptitiously after the marriage. Worse than this, the Attorney-General, who had been hurriedly acquainted with Inspector Dobson's discoveries—until now almost forgotten—elicited the fact that while this intrigue was going on, Madame Barretta was actually under the protection of Sir John Smethurst, who paid for her flat and provided her with nearly all the money she possessed. But though his exposure of this double treachery stripped every shred of decency from the woman in the witness-box, he could not shake her story of the presence of her lover at the Queen Anne's flat on the fatal night. The very depth of her shame added to the general feeling that this woman must be speaking the truth.

The Judge admitted the corroborative evidence of the maid, Janet Kirby. Janet was a dour Scotswoman of fifty. She had been with the Countess Barretta since the latter's return to England after her husband's death. Previously she had been for twenty years with the venerable Marchioness of Sporran. She had been aware of what had been going on between her mistress and Mr. Hastings, but considered it none of her business. She knew nothing about Mr. Hastings' identity, had no curiosity, never read the newspapers, and knew nothing about the present case until suddenly fetched by Mr. Larner, in a taxicab, half an hour previously. But she remembered the date quite well because her mistress had gone away to stay the next day—it might have been at St. Margaret's Lodge ; she thought she remembered being told to forward letters there. Mr. Hastings had come soon after one, and she had heard him leave—her room gave on to the hall—at three. She had no doubts whatever about these facts.

If her mistress's character was frail, Janet's was firm and unshakable as granite, and upon it all the suggestions and insinuations of Sir Horace Stille were instantly and completely shattered.

No other evidence was called. Supplementary addresses were made by the respective counsel—the Attorney-General recording his necessary acceptance, under protest, of his Lordship's ruling—and the Judge shortly summarized the additional evidence.

The jury again retired, as did the Judge and the prisoner. For an hour and a half the court waited in suspense, then his Lordship returned, the prisoner, with bent head, took his stand in the dock, and the jury trooped back into their seats.

The foreman remained standing, and to him the Clerk of Arraigns addressed the customary questions.

" Are you agreed upon your verdict ? "

" We are."

" Do you find the prisoner Guilty or Not Guilty of the charge ? "

" Not Guilty."

" And that is the verdict of you all ? "

" It is."

CHAPTER XXVII

BLINKY TODD

SUPERINTENDENT FRASER and Inspector Dobson left the Old Bailey in gloomy silence, though the reasons for their gloom were diverse. The superintendent was annoyed at the verdict ; he had been confident of getting a conviction. The inspector, on the other hand, was secretly rather pleased that his belief in the innocence of Hastings had been vindicated, but he was deeply shocked—he was a simple soul—by the revelation of his protégé's treachery. It was he, however, who broke the silence.

" Well, that's a rummy go," he said.

The superintendent's answer was a grunt.

" I don't wonder she kept that quiet till the last moment —it about does for her," continued the detective. " She's not got much to thank him for—killing the goose that laid her golden eggs, too."

" You forget the goose was going broke ; there wouldn't have been many more eggs, in any case," commented the superintendent.

174

After a further pause, during which the pair crossed Ludgate Circus, the inspector began again :

" I've never been so mistaken in a man in my life as I have about that chap Hastings. He impressed me all along as a straight, decent fellow—even at first, when I suspected him. I can hardly believe now that he was deceiving that poor girl all the time. I don't know what my missus'll say about it—she's taken a lot of interest in what I've told her about those young people. Well, well ; now we shall have to look round for someone else. What about McCorquodale ? Do you think that ought to be followed up ? "

The pair had now reached the Embankment, and were walking along the pavement next the river where there were few other pedestrians. Before the superintendent could answer his subordinate's question, however, his arm was touched from behind, and a nervous voice said : " Can I 'ave a word with yer, guv'ner ? "

The two police officers stopped and stared at the strange little figure that cringed before them. It was a man little more than five feet high, with long arms and large hands, and a curious flattened head, in which the chief features were a thin, hooked nose and a pair of pale, perpetually blinking eyes. Poor, though not ragged, clothes and a red handkerchief knotted tightly round the throat completed the apparition.

" Well," said the superintendent, " what is it ? "

" It's about that case, guv'ner. I know something about it. Can I 'ave a word, quiet like ? "

" The Hastings case, d'you mean ? "

" That's it, sir."

" You'd better come along to the Yard—here's a tram just coming. Hop in."

But the little man seized him by the arm.

" No, sir," he begged ; " not in there. I couldn't talk to you in there—I'd be that frightened I couldn't speak.

Can't we 'ave it out on one of these benches? It's quiet enough 'ere. It wouldn't do me no good to be seen going in there with you two gents—I've been trying to run straight lately—the 'Army' are 'elping me—an' if they saw me going in there they'd think I was in trouble again."

"All right," said the superintendent, walking to the nearest bench. "Now, then, what's your name?"

"Todd, sir. 'Blinky' Todd, they calls me. I'm known up at your place, though I 'aven't met either of you gentlemen before. What I'm goin' to tell yer'll probably get me into trouble—that's why I didn't tell it before—but I've been followin' this case pretty careful—I've been in court each day—an' I can see if I don't speak up, the wrong chap'll get dropped. You're all on the wrong tack, guv'ner —wrong altergether. But I'd better begin at the start."

Mr. Todd drew the back of his hand across his mouth. He was taking a great risk, and, unconsciously, he felt the need for reinforcement. None, however, was forthcoming, and he continued :

"I'd been watchin' that 'ouse fer some time and had got to know the ways o' the folks. I'd found a winder, too, with a loose catch—scullery winder it was. One night I made up my mind I'd crack it. I went round about eleven —that's a better time to be about than later, 'cos the coppers gets so curious when there's 'ardly anyone about. I meant just to slip into the garden then, and wait there till everyone was asleep before gettin' in. I knew the old man— Smethurst, that is—used sometimes to come out into the garden an' 'ave a walk round, but there was plenty of bushes to 'ide in, an' I noticed 'e never did it after about twelve o'clock. So that night, as 'e didn't come out, I reckoned 'e'd gone to bed early. Oh, I should say as I'd 'ad a narrer squeak gettin' into the gardin. I was just slippin' in at the gate—keepin' an eye up the road fer the copper—when the front door opened an' out came a young chap in evenin' dress. I flopped down in the flower-bed beside the drive—luckily it was in the shadder. 'E stood talkin' to someone at the door for about five minutes, and then 'e come down the drive and out o' the gate without seein' me. I slipped into the bushes and—as I've said—waited there till I thought everyone was asleep. Someone come up to the 'ouse in a taxi not long after, but I couldn't see 'oo it was—I was the other side of the gardin by then.

" Well, at about 'alf-past one I judged they was all asleep an' I made for the scullery winder. The catch was much stiffer than I'd expected—when I got inside I found they'd put on a new one—but I got in and went along the passages till I got to the 'all. It was the study I was makin' fer, 'cos I'd 'eard that the old man kept a pile in 'is safe—these things gets about you know, gentlemen. That 'all was an awkward place—the light was on. I didn't like it a bit. But I knew it was always like that, 'cos I'd seen it through the fan over the door every night I'd bin that way—it didn't mean that anyone was still up. I waited in the passage just outside for what seemed a hour—'spect it was only ten minutes reely. Then I crept across to the study door. I couldn't see in, 'cos there was a key in the lock. I listened an' there wasn't a sound—I've got sharp ears, gentlemen, an' I reckon to 'ear if there's anyone in a room, if they're even sittin' still. I turned the 'andle an' began to push the door open when I see the light was on. That was a nasty shock. I froze for a sec, an' 'eld my breath. Then I began slowly to shut the door, but suddenly I saw somethin' that made me stop sharp. There was a mirrer on the right'and wall, and in it I caught sight of a man sittin' in an arm-chair. At first I thought 'e was asleep, but then I saw that somethin' was up. I thought p'r'aps 'e was taken bad an' I ought to do somethin' for 'im—I'm a soft-'earted bloke, that's bin my trouble all through life."

Mr. Todd paused for an expression of appreciation of

this noble failing, but he only got a " Go on, man," from the superintendent.

" I shoved the door open further an' stuck my 'ead in to make sure there was no one else in the room. There wasn't, so I crep' in and went up to him. It was Smethurst all right. 'E was sittin' in 'is chair on the near side o' the fire-place—with 'is back to the door, that is. 'Is arm was over the side o' the chair with a cigar between the fingers. The cigar 'ad a long ash on it, but it was out—an' so was 'e. 'Is eyes was 'alf shut an' 'is mouth 'alf open, an' there was some blood in 'is ears an' round 'is eyes—inside like. 'E was a 'orrid sight an' 'e was dead as mutton."

" Good God ! " said the inspector. " What time did you say it was ? "

" That must 'ave bin gettin' on for two o'clock, 'cos I'd bin pretty slow gettin' in."

" Two o'clock ! And he was in an arm-chair—dead—not on the floor at all ! Why, that arm-chair—that was the one Hastings said he was sitting in when he left ! Jackson saw him in it, too—someone must have come in and killed him while he was still sitting in it. It must have been McCorquodale, at quarter to twelve, as I said. But—the body—why was it in the chair—how did it get on to the floor by the writing-table—and the telephone—how did it get knocked over, if he was killed in that chair ? "

The superintendent, who had been silent all this time, spoke at last.

" It wasn't McCorquodale. Don't you see, Dobson, that was the very attitude Jackson last saw him in, when he let Hastings out ? *He must have been dead then !* Hastings must have faked it somehow to make it seem as if Sir John was talking to him—easy enough really—and the smoking cigar would give the same impression. Then he must have come back later—after he left the Barretta woman at three—and faked up all that business of the window and the gravel, and the position of the body, and the safe. I don't quite follow the telephone business yet, but I shall. By God, that chap's a clever devil. Look here, Todd, you've got to come on to the Yard whether you like it or not. The Chief's got to hear this story."

He hailed a taxi, and on the way Blinky Todd told how he had been panic-stricken, and escaped from the house as quickly as he could by the way he had come in. He had not dared to tell the police for fear that he should be accused of the crime. Only at the trial had he realized what his silence meant, how in all possibility it might cost an innocent man his life, and he had plucked up courage now to tell his story.

He was very soon telling it again to the Commissioner. Sir James Callender listened to the story in silence, merely nodding from time to time at the interpolated explanations of his subordinates. At the end of the story, he sat back in his chair and stared at Todd.

" You're a nice chap," he said slowly. " If you'd spoken up at the proper time that chap would have been in the condemned cell now, insted of wandering about a free man."

" But, sir, we can get him again—he can't have gone far," broke in the impetuous inspector.

Sir James bent a pitying glance upon him.

" My dear fellow, if Todd had actually seen him hitting Smethurst on the head, we couldn't touch him now. He's been tried and acquitted. He can never be tried again on this charge."

CHAPTER XXVIII

A LETTER TO THE INSPECTOR

" OUTWARD BOUND,
" *December*.

" MY DEAR INSPECTOR,

"Your visit to me on the morning—the rather early morning—after my acquittal, took me rather by surprise, and that, coupled with the not unnatural shock inflicted upon my delicate nerves by your revelation of the adventures of the gentleman of the name of Todd, probably disturbed the nice balance of my judgment. In any case, I did not feel inclined then and there, as you suggested, to write a ' confession ' of my misdeeds. Although I knew well enough that I could not be tried again on the same charge (of that more anon), it seemed too much like putting one's head, in cold blood, into the lion's mouth. Since then I have had time to think things over, and I have changed my mind.

" In the first place I do realize, as you said, that it is rather hard on Sam McCorquodale to have hanging over him the suspicion, which the public would naturally feel, that he was the real ' perpetrator ' and the continual fear that you might be going to charge him—however much you might assure him to the contrary, he would probably think that you were lulling him into a state of false security—as your superintendent kindly did to me. You see how thoughtful I really am for other people's feelings. Secondly, I am just a little bit conceited, and I should rather like you to know how clever I've been over it all. After all, I did defeat Scotland Yard, didn't I? Finally, public opinion being what it is, Geoffrey Hastings will have to disappear in any case, so that a confession of murder more or less will hardly make any difference to him. He hasn't got any relations, so that nobody will really mind, and his wife will be just as happy under another name. So I will unfold the tale :

In the first place, the Crown wasn't too well ' instructed ' about my early history. Or was it deliberately creating a hostile atmosphere by suggesting that I had been brought up in surroundings of security and respectability ? In any case, I let it pass because I did not want to reveal one particular fact about my early life. As a matter of fact, I was never either secure or steady. My father was a clever and ambitious Manchester solicitor. He made a good deal of money—enough to have kept him in reasonable comfort and given me a decent education. But he knew that he could not live long—he was consumptive— and he decided, after my mother's death, when I was still a kid, to live far above his income—on capital, in fact—in order to make me into a ' gentleman.' He sent me to an expensive private school, then to Eton, and finally to Oxford. In my second year there he died. I was left with an expensive education and about two thousand pounds down. I realized—I had a head on my shoulders even then—that that was really nothing, and that I had got to earn my own living. My particular friend at the House was going to be a doctor, and I decided to go in with him. We went on to Bart's and both, in course of time, qualified. But by that time I had developed a weakness that I now recognize as my besetting sin (one can't class murder as a besetting sin, can one ?—it is too incidental)—I can never stick to any one line. I had qualified as a doctor, but I suddenly found that I was tired of it—I simply couldn't settle down to it. So I tried journalism. As usual, I did pretty well—got taken on to the staff of the *Unicorn*, and, just as I was beginning to get tired of that, the owner, Hector Stentorius,

took me on as his secretary. That was a change, and I
settled down to that, and soon there was more change
because Stentorius took up politics and became a pretty
big power in a free-lance sort of way. Then there was the
war, and after that—I'd saved a bit of money by then—I
thought I'd see a bit of the world. I went out to South
America and took up one or two things out there—I needn't
bother you with them—but I couldn't stick to anything,
and I came back in the hope of getting Stentorius to take
me on again—there was always plenty of variety with him.
He couldn't have me—he'd got someone else—but he put
me on to Smethurst and the rest you know—except for
the details.

" I fell in love with Madame Barretta the first time I saw
her at Sir John's house. She was already under his
protection, but as soon as she found out that I was in love
with her she told me all about it—which, I think you'll
agree, was pretty decent of her. It didn't make any
difference to me, though. I don't think I'm particularly
immoral, but I am unmoral, and I have very few principles
outside of a sort of rough and ready sporting code.
Smethurst, although he was generous enough, was pretty
beastly to her, and that made a lot of difference to me later
on. The trouble at the time was that neither of us had got
any money—worth talking about—of our own. I had got
the speculating habit in S. A. and I had dropped a good
deal. I had done better, in a small and safe way, since I
had been with Smethurst, but it wasn't enough to make
any difference. I started plunging again, and unfortunately
she followed my rotten example, and we were soon both
in the soup. I believe you found out that she had been
drawing out fairly big drafts of cash from her bank—she
used to give those to me to settle up her speculation losses.
Things got so desperate that we decided that the only thing
to do was for me to marry Emily Smethurst. At that time
I still thought that Smethurst was a very rich man.

Although, even if Emily would have me—and I thought she would—we couldn't get married soon enough to get Rosamund and me out of our present hole, I calculated that, on the security of our engagement, I could borrow enough for the time being. There I was wrong—the Jews wouldn't look at it—evidently they knew more about Smethurst's affairs than I did and that was the first thing that made me suspicious about his position. When I looked into it—and I could, without much difficulty—I soon found out.

" So I was no better off after my engagement than I was before, and I had lost Rosamund. It was quite untrue that we had agreed to continue our ' liaison,' as they call it, after my marriage to Emily. We had agreed nothing of the kind—that was forced out of Rosamund by that swine Stille—she hardly knew what she was saying. I only tell you that because there's a limit to even my iniquities. Well, there we were—worse off than ever. Then that Rio concession cropped up and I thought I saw the chance of a really big coup. I had a friend in Rio who told me that he was in with the Brazilian Government people ; he said that he could work it so that they should get to hear of Smethurst's position. I felt absolutely convinced that Smethurst wouldn't get the concession, and that McCorquodale would. You know the details of that business. My friend let me down—perhaps intentionally. I had bought Lacecs far beyond my capacity to pay—it meant absolute ruin if they went down—or even if they stayed where they were. Then that Monday I found that letter in my basket. I had been with Smethurst, but had gone back into my room to verify something—our rooms connected. I read it and nearly fainted. All I could do at the moment was to decide not to show him the letter ; I shoved the thing into my pocket, pulled myself together, and went back into his room. He actually asked me about the beastly thing. I told him it hadn't come. I was afraid he might go into the clerk's office when he went out and say something about it, so I told him that I had made inquiries about the S.A. mail, and that it was in all right, and that that meant that if there was a letter from Brazil it would have been delivered by now. All I wanted then was time to think.

" I had just two hours—I was to dine with him at eight. It was the hardest work I have ever done in my life. I was absolutely desperate and absolutely unscrupulous. His having been beastly to Rosamund wiped out any compunction I might have felt. I decided at once that he must never get that concession, and then I sat down in my room at my flat to think out how it was to be done. Within an hour I had the rough outlines of a plan, and before I dressed I had worked in a good many of the details. But a good deal more I had to work out while I was actually dining with him—and that was the hardest work of the lot—not to let him see that I was thinking about something else. Of course, I didn't then work out all the details about my alibi and about getting you people on to the wrong scent —that came bit by bit. But I had all the details for that night worked out, and I sat down to dinner with a candle in my pocket and that little life-preserver in my hip-pocket.

" Now about the plan. You'll probably say that I was taking a prodigious risk—that it was a hundred to one against Jackson being deceived by that faked talk. But as a matter of fact, the odds were really in my favour— that was what made me so confident. You will remember that I had been a medical student (that was the particular fact I didn't want to come out). Well, while I was doing my course, I made a particular study of psychology—I don't mean psycho-analysis, which, I think, is an overdone fad. But psychology proper is at the bottom of all good doctoring, and it interested me more than any other branch. I was particularly impressed by the power of ' suggestion '— there again, I don't mean auto-suggestion, another bit of quackery—but the extraordinary effect that can be made upon an individual—almost any individual—by suggestion of which he is unconscious. It was on that one principle— the power of suggestion—that I based my whole plan, and it ran through the whole thing.

"It was obvious that anyone so closely connected with Smethurst as I was must come under fairly close scrutiny, so that it was essential that I should have an absolutely unshakable alibi. But I have sufficient respect for the C.I.D. to realise that one cannot cook an alibi—that is, that one cannot hoodwink them into thinking that one was in a certain place at a certain time if one really was not. The cooking, therefore, must be done the other way round— the time of the murder must be cooked. That was what I proposed to do, and this is how I did it.

"After dinner, as you know, we went into the study and talked business—some of it was about that Rio concession. You will remember that I told you that I had taken some notes of things he wanted done, especially about artificial silk; well, as a matter of fact, I made those notes after I got home that night, in case you asked to see them—I thought that was rather a clever touch, and I was quite disappointed when you didn't—you ought to have, you know. Actually we didn't touch artificial silk, but I mentioned it because there was an article on it—I marked it— in that copy of the *Financial News*. As soon as Jackson had brought in the drinks and shut the shutters, I made an excuse to get him to the writing-table and then hit him on the back of the head—I knew just where and just how hard to hit—with the life-preserver. I carried him over to the arm-chair next the door and dumped him into it. The first thing I did after that was to pile up a huge coal fire; I wanted to keep his body as warm as possible, so as to delay the stiffening of the limbs—partly so that I could move them into a new position later on, and partly so as to deceive the doctor as to the time the body had been dead.

" Then came the most tricky part of the whole business—arranging that telephone call that was to ' suggest ' the time of the murder. This is how it was done. I put the telephone right on the edge of the desk farthest from the door, tied a piece of string on to the hook, carried the string straight down to near the floor where it ran through the handle of a heavy despatch box. That turned the string from the perpendicular to the horizontal, which was what I wanted. I had, as I said before, brought a candle with me, and this I fastened by its own grease to a book, which I laid on the floor. The string then ran from the despatch box handle straight through the candle, touching the wick, about an inch and a half below the top. From there it went on to the wall, where it was fastened tightly to a pocket-knife that I forced into a crevice in the shutters. When the string was taut I removed the earpiece from the hook. The idea was that the candle, which burns at the rate of roughly an inch an hour, would burn through the string in about an hour and a half's time, when I was safely at my club. The string being severed, the hook of the telephone would automatically fly up and put a call through to the Exchange. Exchange would answer, and, getting no reply, would in all probability—at that hour and on a private line—make a note of the time. When it was all ready, I lit the candle.

" I told you that I had dumped Smethurst into the chair with its back to the door. All I had to do was to arrange him in a natural attitude. I went to the door so as to get the right line of vision ; then I fixed him so that anyone in the hall would see the back of his head (the blow had left no mark that could be seen at that distance), one leg crossed over the other, and one forearm and hand sticking over the arm of the chair. Into the fingers of that hand I put his own cigar which I puffed up into a good glow so that it smoked freely. But I poured a little of the drink from his glass on to the cigar halfway down, to provide against the outside chance of it burning away and marking his fingers. That was what made it smell of whisky.

" Then I rang the bell and opened the door. I stood holding the handle and looking back into the room. As soon as I heard Jackson coming up the stairs I started a conversation with Smethurst, speaking both parts myself. His, of course, was only an inaudible murmur, with a Lancashire inflection—easy enough to do and quite enough to suggest to Jackson that his master was talking. After all, why should he think anything else ? If he had had reason to suspect anything wrong, of course neither that nor the view that he got of Smethurst would have deceived him for an instant. But he had no such reason at all. You know how unobservant people are in the ordinary course of routine. Jackson heard and saw just what he expected to hear and see, and that was quite enough to create the impression in his mind that his master was alive when I left.

" You know my movements after I left the house. I drove to the Club, stayed there till one, walked across to Queen Anne's Flats and stayed there till three. I made a point of leaving just as the clock struck, so that the time could easily be fixed, and I saw to it that we said good-bye outside Janet Kirby's room, so that she should hear it, too. Then I took a taxi to the end of St. John's Road, and walked from there—a couple of minutes' walk—to St. Margaret's Lodge. I had left the study window ajar, and I went in that way. The candle was still burning, though very low. I blew it out and put it and the string and knife and book in my pocket. Then I carried Smethurst's body across and arranged it as you found it. The hands and feet were stiff, but the fire had done its work well, and I was able to move the other limbs into the position I wanted. I rubbed some damp gravel on to the soles of his shoes, and put a little on the carpet behind the curtain where you found it—too much apparently. I took Smethurst's keys out of his pocket and shoved the right one into the lock of the safe—I was working in thin dancing gloves. I also took his memorandum-book, which I thought might have too much in it about the Rio concession. I put Smethurst's cigar, which I left between his fingers, and which had gone out when it reached the part I had wetted, in the ash-tray on the little table by his chair. You asked me once why S. should have left that cigar half-finished—that was why. I didn't notice at the time that a very long ash fell off it when I moved him. I noticed it when I came in with Emily Smethurst in the morning and trod it into powder as I passed—you might have wondered why he hadn't put the ash in the tray by his side, and that might have started you thinking about the attitude in which he was last seen.

" I think that completes what I did in the room—except, of course, that I put the telephone on its side to make it look as if it had been knocked over. It takes a long time to tell, but it only took about ten minutes to do. I slipped out the way I had come in and made for home—and bumped into that scavenger fellow, Flush. That might have done me in, but, by tremendous luck, it helped me a lot, because he said he had seen me at two. What he actually heard was the clock striking half-past three—you know how the quarters strike on many clocks, one, two, or three single strokes. As I went along I tore the written pages out of Smethurst's memorandum-book, and shoved the book itself deep into a dustbin. I burnt the pages in my grate when I got home and floated the ashes out of the window. After putting back the life-preserver and making up those notes I told you about, I went to bed.

" That was the first part of my job. The second was really much more subtle. I saw that if I was really suspected I must at all costs divert attention from the time *before* I left the house. Jackson's impression of having seen his master alive, then, might have broken down under close questioning. So I deliberately excited your suspicion about my alibi—I misled you into thinking that I had taken a taxi off the rank in Blenheim Road. I knew I could always put that right when I wanted to—I had the chap's number, though I told you I hadn't—and I trusted that the clearing up of that point, together with the proof of the infallibility of my alibi as a whole, would be enough to clear me. But in case it didn't, I had to play a much more dangerous game. I hoped that the doctors would fix a fairly small limit round about twelve o'clock—remember that the tremendous heating I gave the body was bound to make them late in their estimate. But in case they extended their limits, I had to draw your attention to the *late* rather than the *early* limit—to 2 a.m. rather than 10 p.m. Therefore I deliberately made up a very weak and suspicious false alibi after 1 a.m. I had, of course, a real alibi for that period—1 to 3 a.m.—but I could not produce it at that stage, because you would then at once have turned your attention to the *early* limit.

" So, when I was arrested, and all through my various trials, I said nothing about my real one to three alibi—with Madame Barretta. I kept it up my sleeve—by arrangement with her—until the very last moment, when it would be too late for you to turn your attention to the early period. There was a chance, of course, that the Judge wouldn't admit the evidence, but when things reached that stage I had to take chances. So you see that my theory of ' suggestion ' ran through the whole thing, and, considering I had to make it up on the spur of the moment, I don't think it was a very bad effort. Anyhow, you all, one after the other, fell into my successive suggestion traps, and I am now a free man—immune from all further fear on that charge.

" Of course, I am a bad lot—but not quite so bad as the story sounded. Smethurst was a bully when he had people in his power—as he had Madame Barretta. He was a beast to her, and I can't regret killing him. I certainly behaved badly to Emily Smethurst, but she won't break her heart over me—she was a cold-blooded little fish, really. And I have already told you that it was untrue that we had planned to go on—Rosamund and I—after my marriage to Emily. What might have happened, I don't know—that was on the knees of the gods.

"Of course, too, I am a ruined man—as Geoffrey Hastings. But I have my not inconsiderable wits and the best wife a man could hope for, and I have no fear about the future. We are, as you see at the top of this letter, 'outward bound' for our new life. It's no use your looking at the postmark, because that's not where we're going. I am sending this letter to a 'trusty friend' in Australia—he will put it in a new envelope and post it to you next time he is in some big city. You will get it months after we have arrived somewhere else—so you can't trace us even if you want to.

"One last word. I want you to believe this : my wife— she will be my wife by the time you get this—was in no way my accomplice ; she knew nothing whatever about what I had done until I found that you—or, rather, your fat friend—were hot on my trail. Then I had to tell her, to get her help about the late alibi. It was a horrible shock to her, but she has stuck to me and I shan't let her down.

"I am afraid I was a little bit of a shock to you, Inspector. You were very good to me and, I think, rather believed in me. That makes me feel rather a worm. But the worm, you will admit, put up a good fight.

> "Yours apologetically,
> "GEOFFREY HASTINGS (ci-devant)."

"P.S.—On reading this through, I find there is one point on which I haven't enlightened you. You must want to know how one of McCorquodale's cigarettes came to be in the tray on Smethurst's writing-table. If I tell

ou that I had it in my case by accident, you will probably
ot believe me. And if it was not by accident, then it
must mean that I had put it there; and later put it in that
sh-tray, with the intention of throwing suspicion on
McCorquodale. That implies premeditation and destroys
all that I have said about ' the spur of the moment.' Well,
I will be honest with you, Inspector, for the nonce. I did
have some vague idea about doing this, at the back of
my mind, for some weeks before the letter came. And I
thought it might be useful to throw suspicion on someone
else. So I took an opportunity to purloin one of poor
Sam's cigarettes, in case of accident. Perhaps I have
treated him rather badly, but I've made the *amende
honorable* now, haven't I ?

" G. H."

BIOGRAPHY
and MEMOIRS

DARK BLUE COVERS